HOMICIDE IN THE HILLS

Drug dealers. Hookers. Pimps. Gangsters. Welcome to Hollywood.

His ex-wife hates him. He's got a kid he never sees. For Detective Salvador Reyes, newest member of the Hollywood Precinct homicide team, life is murder ... and murder is about to become his life. A porn-film director is beaten to death in an attack so savage that Reyes is convinced there's more to this killing than meets the eye. Soon he's drawn deep into the underbelly of Tinseltown, in all its tarnished glory.

HOMICIDE IN THE HILLS

HOMICIDE IN THE HILLS

by

Steve Garcia

Dales Large Print Books
Long Preston, North Yorkshire,
BD23 4ND, England.

British Library Cataloguing in Publication Data.

Garcia, Steve
    Homicide in the hills.

    A catalogue record of this book is
    available from the British Library

    ISBN   978-1-84262-739-6 pbk

First published in Great Britain in 2008 by Black Star Crime

Copyright © Working Partners 2008

Cover illustration © David Irvine by arrangement with
Arcangel Images

The moral right of the author has been asserted

Published in Large Print 2010 by arrangement with
Harlequin Enterprises II B.V./S.à.r.l.,

Dales Large Print is an imprint of Library Magna Books Ltd.

Printed and bound in Great Britain by
T.J. (International) Ltd., Cornwall, PL28 8RW

With special thanks to Peter Welling

To all those who contributed in their own
way, especially:
Darlene F, Michael D, Sara Grant, Kim
Utterson, Chris Wuensch and the Back
Room at NDNation

Prologue

Salvador Reyes' cousin once told him that there once was a law on the books in Texas that said 'you could kill a man if he needed a'killin''. Reyes wondered if a Californian judge would accept that explanation if he shot his landlord, Mr. Bognár.

Por favor your honor, there I was, sweating my cojones off because the damn air conditioner broke again, and the guy didn't care. I mean, that was the third time this summer, your honor. I figured that son-of-a-bitch deserved killing.

Reyes parked his bike outside Walgreen's Drug Store. He headed straight to the cooler and plucked out a bottle of water.

The short, matronly clerk smiled. 'How are you today?'

Let's see... I woke up at 4:00 am, soaked in my own sweat. I have to face my ex before I can pick up my son later. Oh, and three, my day off has vanished in a phone call. Thanks for asking.

'Fine,' he said.

'Have a good one,' she said as she handed him his receipt and change.

'You, too.' He stepped outside, opened the water, took a sip, then rubbed the plastic bottle across his forehead. According to

Weather Girl Glenda, it was going to be a scorcher today, and his new vinyl cycling suit was fast becoming a sauna in the morning sun. He straddled his bike and checked his watch. It was 6:10 am.

A police cruiser slowed down, pulled over to the curb and stopped. A uniformed officer stepped from the car and pointed at Reyes. 'Don't move. Hold it right there.' He reached into his pocket and put on a pair of sunglasses. 'Ah, that's better. Between the sun and your shiny clown suit, I damn near went blind.'

'Hey, that's some funny shit, Joe,' Reyes said. 'See how hard I'm laughing?'

'Jesus H. Cheesecake, what in the hell are you wearing?' said Officer Donawald. 'You know, if you put on a red Afro and some large red shoes, you could start selling Big Macs.'

'Speaking of clowns, how's your life?'

'Life's a bitch and so is the wife,' Donawald said. 'Want to put your bike in the trunk?'

'Yeah. Can you drop it off at the station later? I'll need it to get home tonight.'

'Sure, although, everything considered, I kind of figured you for a unicycle.'

'Just open the damned truck.'

Donawald popped the latch and helped put the bike inside. 'Ready?'

'Let's go,' Reyes said.

'So, what's the story here?' Donawald

asked as he pulled away from the curb. 'I was told to pick you up and bring your ass up to the Hills. Of course, I was expecting you to be in plain clothes but obviously I was wrong.' He laughed again.

'First of all, this is an exercise suit, okay?'

'That is not *just* an exercise suit. It's a very, very yellow exercise suit.'

'As for what the hell is going on,' Reyes said. 'I don't know. Wallace knows it's my day off but she called and says she's got a homicide up there and needs me. They're short-handed. I know I'm the junior guy, but it's my kid's birthday today. If I don't show up to take him out to dinner, my ex will rip me a new one.'

'That sucks, man,' Donawald said. 'Don't they have enough people to cover one homicide?'

'They've got five or six, depending on what else they have to do. But they haven't replaced Rodriguez and Wayman's retired. I mean, the Captain isn't going out but he could cover shit at the station and free up somebody else.'

'Who's the stiff? Anybody famous?'

'Hell, I don't know. Phil didn't say. Isn't everybody who lives there famous?'

'It depends how far up or down the Hill you go,' Donawald said. 'This address? It's near the bottom, my friend.'

The two men made small talk as they

13

headed to the crime scene. Reyes' thoughts wandered to his son, Fernando. He was seven years old today and Reyes would get to see him for exactly three hours, from five till eight. Pam would make sure it wasn't a minute more or a minute less. The court's decisions on the property settlement and on visitation had been so unfair, so one-sided, that Reyes often wondered if Pam's father had bribed the judge. And of course, Pam wouldn't budge an inch on anything. She adhered to the letter of the divorce decree, each paragraph and sub-paragraph. Two weeks ago the Captain gave him two tickets to the Dodgers, a last-minute thing, and he called Pam to see if he could pick up Nando and take him to the ballpark for the day. 'Oh no. No way,' she'd said. 'No visits are scheduled. It's not your day to have him.'

Por favor your honor...

1

Philippa Wallace pushed her way through the throng of media toward the yellow crime scene tape and the waiting uniformed offi-cers. Ahead was Joan Quaker from Channel 2 – a long-time pain in the ass – and her equally obnoxious cameraman Rey-Rey.

Quaker shoved a microphone in her face. 'Detective Wallace, can you tell us what's going on in there?'

Wallace ignored the question as she cut a swath through the reporters and their entourages. Questions bombarded her.

'How many victims?'

'Do you have any names?'

'I heard that a well-known movie star was killed. Is that true?'

'How about suspects?'

'People, people.' Wallace said. She held up her hands to signal for silence. 'At least let me get inside and take a look around before you start misquoting me, will you?'

'How long do you think it will be before you have something for us?' Richard Deems of Fox asked. '*Morning News* is cranking up.'

'I'd love to help you, Mr. Deems, but I really should go check things out before I start issuing statements. I'll bring you up to speed as soon as I can.'

Wallace turned. The media members continued to hurl questions after her.

'Good morning,' she said, greeting the officers guarding the entrance to the grounds of the property. 'Early start today, huh?'

Several of the officers muttered something as she passed. It may have been greetings, maybe not. It didn't matter any more than Sal's pissing and moaning did. She had a job to do and she had to do it with resources

15

that were available.

She paused to size up the house. It was typical for the neighborhood, a little up on a midsize, with salmon stucco walls, a tiled roof, and plenty of palm trees, bushes and flowers that were most likely tended to by a gardener. To the left was a carport large enough to accommodate two vehicles, but there was only one car in it and it was under a cover.

A redwood pergola sat about halfway between the house and the carport. It was smothered by purple bougainvillea. In the midst of all that purple, Wallace spotted the blue of a uniformed officer, another new female face. Had to be a rookie. A woman sat beside her, hugging a little girl to her. Wallace nodded to the group, said good morning and introduced herself.

'Good morning,' the officer replied.

'You new to the district?' Wallace asked.

'Yes, ma'am. My second week. Officer Tripucka.'

'Welcome aboard. Who do we have here, Tripucka?'

'This is Manuela Cortez,' Tripucka said, gesturing to the petite Hispanic woman next to her, who was nervously rocking the little girl. 'She was the victim's house-cleaner. The little girl is her daughter, Sara. Mrs. Cortez discovered the body when she came to work this morning. She called nine-one-one. We found her outside on the porch.'

'Uh-huh. What time did she start work today?'

'Six o'clock.'

'Did she tell you how she got in?'

'She has her own keys. She went into the kitchen and found the victim.'

Wallace nodded. 'How many days a week does she come in?'

'Five. Monday through Friday.'

'Damn, how dirty can the place get? If I cleaned my house that often, my husband would think I was crazy. Of course, if he cleaned it even once I'd figure he was up to something.' She shrugged and turned back to the woman and her daughter. There was fear in Mrs. Cortez' face as her gaze flitted between them. Wallace glanced at the little girl, who stared back with large, vacant, chocolate-colored eyes. 'Are you okay? Is your daughter okay?'

Mrs. Cortez pulled Sara a little closer. 'No,' she said, and shook her head. 'I don't know.' She was obviously struggling, searching for the right words.

She has limited English,' Tripucka said. 'Between what she does know and my high school Spanish we've been able to get by.'

'You're not trained as an interpreter?'

'No, ma'am.'

'Why didn't somebody call for one?' Wallace asked.

17

'*Mi hija...*' Mrs. Cortez shook her head. 'My daughter. *Vaminos?* You know *vaminos?* Um. We ... um ... we go now to ... *mi casa* ... *mi* house? *Sí, sí,* my house?'

Detective Wallace smiled. 'Um, *una momento.*' She held up one finger and then looked at Tripucka.

'It's actually *un momento,*' the officer said.

'I think she understood me,' Wallace said. 'Do you have a statement from Mrs. Cortez?'

'Sergeant Blaylock took one.'

'Without an interpreter?'

'Well...'

'Look. You stay with Mrs. Cortez. I'm going to talk to Blaylock.'

Detective Wallace headed toward the house without waiting for a response. She stopped to check out footprints marked by eight yellow tent cards. Her first guess was that they were blood. They started on the porch and disappeared, as the individual who made them apparently left the path and crossed the grass.

The front door to the house was open. Sergeant Blaylock was standing in the foyer talking on his radio. Wallace carefully stepped inside, avoiding the footprints on the marble tiles. She checked her reflection in the hall mirror. *Oh, man,* she thought. *Now I know why I don't use hundred-watt bulbs in my bathroom. I look like hell.*

The bright light caused the silver curls in her black hair to sparkle. Oh, she knew she would never be mistaken for Tyra Banks, or even Oprah for that matter, but she sure as hell didn't want to be taken for her Grandmother Aurora. Wallace twisted her head and studied the deep furrows that creased her eyes and forehead. 'Damn,' she said, then caught herself. Making sure no one had heard her, she turned to examine the foyer.

She ran her finger over the glass-top table beneath the mirror and left a streak in the dust. *Odd,* she thought. She pulled out her notebook.

'Hi, Phil. How are you?' Sergeant Blaylock said.

'Old and slow,' she said. 'Whatcha got here?'

'The victim is a white male, twenty-eight. His name is Zane Kowalski. I think he used to have a face before somebody beat it to a bloody pulp. I mean, it's hamburger-bad.'

'Okay, I think I've got the picture. What else?'

'It might have been a burglary gone wrong. Besides the kitchen, the only room that yielded anything was his bedroom. His wallet was lying on a dresser with some credit cards in it but no cash. There was some bling-bling lying around but mostly it appeared to be that gaudy faux shit. There were cigarette butts in the ashtray and an unconsumed drink by the DVD player. The player was on and the drawer was open, but no DVD. I'm guessing he was about to put in a movie and hit the sack. The bed wasn't slept in, though, so I'm thinking he probably surprised an intruder about that time.'

'Uh-huh. Any evidence that there was a forced entry?'

'There are some marks on the French doors in the kitchen. Definitely looks like someone may have tried to force the lock,' Blaylock said. 'However, the doors were locked when we got here. Everything else looked okay.'

'How about that security camera outside above the door? Any chance we have anything on film?'

'The system was being installed. It isn't connected.' Blaylock handed Detective Wallace a set of keys. 'I took these from the house-cleaner, a Hispanic woman...'

'Yeah, I saw her outside. Did you see if she's got a Green Card?'

'She didn't have it on her. I'm running her now but she says she and her husband are both legal. I think she's more worried about convincing us of that than about her employer being murdered.'

'And despite policy, you took her statement without using an interpreter?'

Blaylock jerked back. He stared into Wallace's accusing eyes. 'One of the new officers assigned to me can speak some Spanish.'

'Uh-huh. I spoke to her. She's not certified. You could have gotten your balls in a wringer. Post-Porter case rules, Sarge. You know that.'

Sergeant Blaylock hesitated before responding. 'Okay.' His buddy-buddy tone had been dialed down a notch. 'Do you want to hear the rest?'

Detective Wallace sighed. 'Yes.'

'It appears that Mrs. Cortez came to work, found the dead body and like a good citizen – or not – called the police.'

'Do we know why her kid is here?'

'She told me that she and her husband both work but can't afford daycare. Apparently Kowalski didn't care if Mrs. Cortez brought the little girl along.'

'Do you know where her husband works?'

'Yeah,' Blaylock said. He flipped through his notes. 'It's the Jonathan Laird Boat Works on Sepulveda.'

'Hmm. Okay. Well, let's make finding out their alien status a priority. Since we don't know who we're looking for yet, we might want to assure ourselves that one of the possible suspects isn't going to flee the country, if you get my drift.'

'Do you really think that she...'

'Not likely, but we don't have much info yet. Oh, and when you check on her status, do so in a way that means we aren't accused of profiling, will you, please? I don't need to be dealing with any of that BS.'

'Sure. PC all the way. Like I said, though, we're already running her and it's strictly by the book.'

'I assume the M.E. has been called?'

'Yup. I'm waiting for him and forensics. They should be here any second.'

'Let me take a peek at the body before they get here.'

Blaylock and Wallace checked out the hallway first. He pointed to the smeared footprints and a handprint on the wall. 'He obviously was having trouble running, what with all that blood on his shoes.'

Wallace examined a handprint on the wall. 'Looks like he was wearing gloves. The print's too smeared to do us much good I'd imagine.'

Blaylock led the way into the kitchen, to a space between the kitchen island on his right and the cabinets and counter on his left.

'There's what's left of him.'

Wallace's eyes ran up from a pair of lifeless feet to bare legs, a pair of black Calvin Klein shorts, and a toned, blood-flecked torso. Zane Kowalski was flat on the Italian marble floor He was face up, except that his face was gone.

'Holy shit,' she said.

2

Blood, bone and brain were all over the floor and cabinets. Something that might have been an eyeball rested under a vegetable tray. There were even some splatters on the ceiling. Turning from the gory sight, Wallace took in the situation as calmly as possible. *Who could do that to a person?* Blood had pooled where Kowalski's limbs were touching the ground. She stepped back and swallowed drily.

'There's no blood on the refrigerator,' she said. 'The first splatters appear on the countertop right next to it. So he got into the kitchen before he was taken down. I'm guessing he took one in the back of the head. That probably dropped him here where the attacker finished the job.'

'So he probably came down and someone surprised him in the kitchen?'

'I think so. Of course, I didn't look around yet but I would assume you would have mentioned it if you had seen blood elsewhere in the house, right?'

'You bet. You know me, Phil, always by the book. That's why they call me By-the-Book Blaylock.'

23

'No one calls you that.'

'They should.'

'Blaylock, you are so full of shit.' Wallace rubbed two fingers over her lips as she studied the crime scene. 'I'm guessing those to be the killer's bloody footprints. They're too big for the housekeeper's but you already checked her shoes, right?'

'If we're guessing, then yeah, I'd say so. And yes, we checked the Cortez woman's shoes. They're clean.'

'We're going to need photos,' Wallace said. 'Maybe we can come up with the make of the intruder's shoes.'

'Photos? Gee, I wish I had thought of that. I sure hope Lewis brings his camera.'

'Smart-ass.'

'Yeah, well.'

'I'm going to take a look around,' Wallace said, secretly glad to be leaving the corpse behind. *Men and cops. Neither ever changed.*

Peals of laughter came from the front of the house.

'What the hell is that noise?' asked Wallace.

'I don't know,' Sergeant Blaylock said. 'Media stampede?'

'Damn, I hope not. They've been on us like dogs in heat trying to find another Porter case. I don't need any leg-humping sons-of-bitches this early in the morning.'

The two police officers stepped back out through the front door.

'Oh my God,' Blaylock said. 'Well, I see it but I still don't know what the hell it is.'

Wallace watched as Reyes made his way through the media crush, then past his fellow officers. He was easy to spot. He looked like a giant, lemon Popsicle. His picture, in that outfit, would be on the morning news, which Deputy Chief Murray would surely be watching. She sighed. 'It's my partner.'

'No shit,' Blaylock said, already laughing like the rest of the uniforms. 'Hey, Sal, can you turn off your clothes, please? I left my suntan lotion in the cruiser.'

One of the officers near the entrance to the driveway shouted, 'I'm blind, I'm blind.'

Detective Reyes made his way across the lawn to the front steps. 'Funny guys,' he said. Then he turned back toward the street and shouted, 'They're looking for a replacement for Leno, you know.'

Reyes stood on the steps for a moment staring at Wallace and Blaylock who were both grinning. 'Now, don't you start with me, too, Phil.'

'What? I didn't do anything.'

'You called me in on my day off. You didn't even give me time to change.'

Wallacc managed to suppress her smile, but the other officers burst out laughing again. Reyes turned and flipped them the bird. 'Can we go inside now? If I wanted abuse I could go see my ex, which, by the way, I have to do at five.' He turned toward the pergola, where Manuela Cortez was still sitting with little Sara. 'Suspect?'

'House-cleaner,' Blaylock said. 'And her daughter.'

'That suit zap mosquitoes?' Blaylock asked. 'He's here all week, folks,' Reyes said.

'Well, I'd love to continue but here comes Doctor Tom,' Blaylock said. He headed down the driveway to greet the medical examiner.

Wallace and Reyes turned and headed to the kitchen. 'Doc's going to want us out of his way,' Wallace said, 'but take a look, then you can help me check the rest of the house.'

'Aw, crap,' Reyes said, his face creasing, when he got his first look at the remains. 'You know, you could warn a guy.' He studied the body of Zane Kowalski. 'He's got bruising on his arms and upper chest. Defensive wounds probably. Face saw better days.'

'Did you also notice the bruise on the right knee?' Wallace asked. 'That may have been one of the first blows. I think the one that made sure he stayed down was to the head.' She pointed out the splatters near the refrigerator.

Reyes nodded, then leaned over for a closer look at the front of the cabinets and island. 'There are some marks here where the killer might have swung and missed. There's some damage under the countertop and to the face of the drawers. Maybe foren-

26

sics can dig out some trace evidence to identify the type of weapon used.'

'Yeah, we'll let them take it from here. Come on.' They passed Dr. Tom Hackett in the hallway. 'I think the cause of death may be easy on this one, Doc,' Wallace said.

'Hello, Detectives,' Dr. Hackett said. He stopped dead in his tracks, stared at Reyes for a minute, then moved toward the body.

'Hold it,' said Lewis Drake, the forensic photographer. He snapped a photo of Wallace and Reyes. 'Thanks. The boys outside wanted a souvenir shot.' He slipped past the two detectives and into the kitchen.

'Come on,' Wallace said. She briefed him on what little she knew about the crime as they stepped into the living room. 'Kowalski was not exactly an interior decorator.'

'So I see. White walls, black leather furniture...'

The living-room ceiling was open to the second-floor, which allowed a view of the upstairs. The floors were hardwood and highly polished. Wallace walked over to a glass-and-chrome end table. She ran her finger over the glass. 'If Mrs. Cortez comes in five days a week, why is everything dusty?'

'Maybe Kowalski has a dirty hobby.'

'More likely Mrs. Cortez hasn't been cleaning lately.'

'She cleans every weekday. Isn't that what you said?'

'Well, she comes to work but what does she do when she gets here? She's pretty cute. Did you see her outside?'

'I didn't get a good look. She seemed kind of small. You think she's fooling around? Hell, you said she's got her daughter with her. She isn't going to, you know, do that in front of her kid.'

'You can never under-estimate the stupidity of parents,' Wallace said. 'Mrs. Cortez could plop her kid in front of a television or something. If she's an illegal, maybe Kowalski threatened to report her if she didn't agree to give him a little action.'

'I don't see it,' Reyes said. 'Kowalski looked like he put his face in the waste disposal. No five-feet-two female could do that.'

'You're probably right. I was thinking out loud. Let's check the rest of the first floor before we go upstairs.'

The two detectives walked down another hall. Reyes opened a door on the right and found a small bathroom. 'The can is clear. Pretty sterile.'

Wallace nodded. 'Let's see what's behind door number two.' She threw open a door on the left.

'Alright,' she said. 'Looks like we found Kowalski's games room. Let's see what kind of games he played.'

The room was painted off-white with burgundy carpeting, except for a bar area in the far corner. To their left was an entertainment unit with three rows of stadium seating in front of an enormous flatscreen TV. A deep rose-colored curtain could be drawn to provide a theater atmosphere and darken the viewing area.

Reyes whistled. 'That's some TV!'

In the center of the room was a pool table, covered in a purple velour sheet. A Tiffany lamp stood on a nearby side table. Wallace pulled back the corner of the velour sheet.

'I'm going to guess the lamp is a fake,' she said.

'Maybe,' Reyes said. 'Maybe not.' He was inspecting a row of pictures on the wall. 'This lithograph is a signed LeRoy Neiman.'

'How about the other one?' Wallace asked as she checked out what looked like an arcade machine.

'Hell, it's one of Patrick Nagel's. He used to be an artist for *Playboy* back in the seventies or eighties. These have to be worth a few coins.'

'You into that kind of stuff?' Wallace asked.

'I saw some of his stuff in a gallery. Out of my league dollar-wise, of course.'

'With all the video games available today, why would anyone want a pinball machine?' Wallace asked. 'And then why would you unplug it?' She reached down and plugged it in. Nothing. 'I guess it's broken.'

Reyes joined Wallace. 'It's an early Pac-

Man unit. I bet a collector would love it.'

'So our boy had some money it seems. Let's go check the bar,' Wallace said as they walked toward the noncarpeted area of the room. 'Looks like it's supposed to be a small dance floor,' she said as they crossed the tiled area surrounding a curved wooden bar, its front covered in thick leather padding.

Wallace stood behind the bar. Reyes stopped a few feet short, and looked down. 'The floor feels a little sticky.'

'Just something else that hasn't been cleaned.' She reached in her pocket and pulled out a pair of latex gloves. 'Most of the booze isn't open,' she said as she lifted one of the bottles on the bar. 'Except this one – Rey Sol Anejo tequila,' she said. 'Its half-empty. So is the margarita mix.'

'It looks like dusting isn't the only thing the cleaning lady missed. Check this out.'

Wallace squatted next to Reyes. 'What is it?'

'Glass.'

Reyes picked up a few shards and collected them in his palm. They were different colors. The carpet was badly stained where it met the tiles.

'They had a pretty decent spill here of some kind,' said Wallace.

Reyes sniffed the carpet. 'Alcohol?'

'Mark this area. We'll have forensics check the stain and the glass. Maybe there's enough to identify the source.'

They moved to the corner of the room opposite the bar where an enameled black *shoji* screen provided privacy for a small office area. Keyes sat down and rummaged through the drawers while Wallace checked the folders and loose papers on the desk.

Suddenly Reyes sat bolt upright. 'Hey, Phil, what's missing from this picture?'

'What're you talking about?' Wallace asked.

'Where the hell is the computer? I'm no geek but based on the number of wires lying here,' he said, holding up several, 'I'd say there should be a computer and a monitor hooked to the other end of two of these. Considering how many there are, I suspect that there was probably a scanner and a printer, and maybe a camera, too.'

'The kind of stuff a thief might take to make a little drug money.'

'I can't believe that whatever they took was worth dying for,' Reyes said, 'or killing for.'

'People have been killed for a lot less. Let's see if we can find out exactly what's missing. For all we know it might not have been stolen. Maybe he moved it or sold it.'

'I'll check it out.'

Wallace headed up upstairs and Reyes followed. The bedrooms were sparsely furnished, with little in the way of decoration.

Reyes opened the closet door. 'Hey. All of the paintings and stuff are in here.'

Wallace checked it out. 'That's weird. A

clock. Paintings. Sconces. Why not put them up?'

The only room that looked used was the master bedroom. The bed appeared to have been readied for sleeping. The mint-green comforter and lavender sheets were turned down but no one had slept in the bed. The sheets were crisp and taut.

'What do you suppose made those marks?' Wallace asked, pointing to three indents in the carpet. They formed a triangle, the dents equally spaced.

'A tripod?' Reyes said, stating the obvious. He looked at Wallace to see if she agreed. She nodded, not saying a word. 'Oh,' Reyes said. 'Oh.'

'Forensics can take this glass and the ashtray but I'm betting they came from Kowalski,' Wallace said. 'Blaylock said there was no DVD in the player. I don't see one lying around, either. You know, like he was about to play it.'

'Phil, I'm ready to head out,' Dr. Hackett yelled from the bottom of the stairs.

Wallace and Reyes headed back to the kitchen where they joined Dr. Hackett, Lewis Drake and two technicians who stood by with a gurney.

'If you folks don't need the late Mr. Kowalski anymore, I'm moving him out,' Dr. Hackett said. 'At least, as much of him as I can. Do you need another look?'

'I think we've seen enough,' Wallace said. 'So?'

Dr. Hackett nodded to his assistants to remove the body. He waited until they placed the mortal remains of Zane Kowalski in a body bag, hefted it onto the gurney, carefully maneuvered around the blood and the detectives, and headed for the ambulance. Drake proceeded to take a few more photos.

'Obviously I've not run any tests yet,' Dr. Hackett said, 'but the initial look-see suggests the victim died of blunt-force trauma to the head. Pick a spot, any spot.'

'Got a time?' Wallace asked.

'Let's see. A rough guess on the time of death? Based on the onset of livor mortis, I'd say between midnight and two.'

'Okay, thanks Doc. That it?'

'That's it for now. I'll call you when I finish running the tests.'

After Hackett left, Wallace fished in her pockets for Manuela Cortez' keys and threw them to Reyes. 'Take a look at those back doors,' she said. 'Blaylock said there was evidence of forced entry.'

Reyes opened the doors and checked the area around the lock and the bolt. 'Yeah. Jimmy marks. Somebody definitely tried getting in without a key. File marks on the metal, gouges in the wood. Was it locked when the cleaner arrived?'

'Apparently so,' said Wallace. 'Maybe the

killer locked them afterwards.'

'Well, it wasn't Kowalski,' said Reyes. 'You want me to look around outside?'

'Sure,' said Wallace. 'I'll finish up here.'

3

Reyes stepped out onto an old, vine-covered, four-column portico and surveyed the pool area. It smacked of days gone by and, oddly enough, of the house his ex-father-in-law had purchased for him and Pam as a wedding present. Old man Vander Bosch despised Reyes but he wanted his daughter and grandchild to live well.

Reyes shook himself from the grip of an ugly past. A quick walk around the pool revealed nothing out of the ordinary. He waved at a couple of the officers who were busy searching through the bushes. 'What are you looking for?' he asked.

'Murder weapon,' one of them replied. 'Want to help?'

'Thanks, no. I'm not much with flowers.'

Reyes headed for the L-shaped pool-house, which appeared to be a mini-replica of a Roman temple. He tried a number of keys in the double doors before finding the right one.

Inside it was rather spartan, with a white-tiled floor and a bare bulb hanging in a narrow hallway with four doors on one side. He checked the first three to reveal changing rooms and a supply closet that contained cleaning materials. At the end was a small kitchen. He found no food, just drinks. There was booze of all sorts, as well as soft drinks, mixers, beer, wine. It was a goddam liquor store. The beer was all the high-priced stuff. He was tempted to grab a cold one, in spite of the early hour, but decided against it.

At the end of the hallway the corridor turned a corner and Reyes found a green door. He turned the knob, then felt suddenly vulnerable. He tapped lightly on the door with the back of his knuckles. 'Police,' he said softly.

No answer. *I wish I had my nine-millimeter,* he thought. Slowly, he pushed open the door. It was dim and he fumbled along the wall with his hand until he found a switch.

'Da-amn!' he whispered as the lights came on. The room was a tech center. A built-in table with numerous surge control plugs ran the length of the room along the far wall. There were two PCs and two Macs, brand-new, still in their boxes, along with film editing equipment, audio recorders, cameras, tripods, and more. A literal film factory sprawled before him.

Next to one of the PCs was new video-editing software. Power Director. Nero. The latest versions. Kowalski was cutting edge.

Along the wall on the right were several dark gray cabinets. He opened the first cabinet. It was full of porn.

'Madre de Dios!'

DVDs, VCR tapes – you name it, Kowalski had it.

Reyes rummaged through the triple-x material. *Suck This. Suck This Too. Goodfellatios.*

Then he pulled open the second cabinet. There were stacks of plastic storage trays. He took one out and removed the top. All sorts of sexually oriented paraphernalia. Toys. Dildos. French Ticklers. He picked up a boxed-up dildo: 'Bonerfied. Practice Makes Perfect.'

Reyes moved to the last cabinet. Boxes and labels. The infamous plain-brown-wrapper shipping department.

Shaking his head, Reyes returned to the house and found Wallace and Blaylock standing by the front door. 'You might want to come with me and check out the poolhouse,' he said.

'You look pale.'

'Let's say that Kowalski's hobbies are a little far-out for a good Catholic boy like me.'

Wallace gave him a puzzled look, but she and Blaylock followed him back to the poolhouse.

'Holy shit,' Blaylock said as he scanned the pornography studio. 'Who'd have guessed?'

Wallace looked around. She picked up a string of Ben-Wa balls, then threw them back into the drawer. 'Get all of this stuff boxed up and sent to the station, will you, Sarge?'

'Who gets the tough assignment of sorting through it?' Blaylock asked. 'I'm no Siskel and Ebert but I'll do it if no one else is available. Hell, I'll even work overtime if needed.'

'Yeah, yeah, funny,' Wallace said. 'Thanks for volunteering but I think I'll give it to our resident porn experts for a once-over.'

'Who's that?' Blaylock asked.

'Kahn and Wagner.'

4

'Wake *up.*'

Donald Kahn heard Angie's Splenda-sweet voice a few seconds before she pinched his big toe. 'You'll be late for work.'

Kahn pulled his foot back under the sheet, then raised his head a few inches off the pillow and smiled. 'I could make you late for work, too.'

'You need to get up. That partner of yours will be here soon. He'll blow his horn and the Goldbergs will blow their gaskets.'

'Come back to bed,' Kahn mumbled.

'It's tempting, but my students await. I'll see you tonight. You be careful at the office.' She gave him a kiss. 'Seriously now, get up. I don't want Harlen waking our neighbors.'

After she'd gone Kahn slipped out of bed, grabbed the remote from the nightstand and clicked on the local news.

Weather Girl Glenda was pointing at the map. 'We'll have clear skies but it will be a hot one today, a real scorcher. Make sure you use a good sunscreen that has an SPF of at least thirty. Drink plenty of fluids, non-alcoholic, unless you're at a party, and then remember to invite me...'

Kahn showered, found a slightly wrinkled short-sleeved shirt and grabbed his lucky tie. It was lucky because it was the one he was wearing the night he met Angie. She had commented about the unusual pattern. He said it was a stylized Gila monster and somehow that intrigued her.

Angie had stocked the refrigerator. Unfortunately, that meant tofu, veggies or fruit – pick one, any one. *What I wouldn't give for a stack of pancakes soaking in Mrs. Butterworth's and a side of bacon,* he thought.

The timer on the coffeepot beeped. He poured a mug, gave it a cooling puff or two and then took a couple of sips. Angie suggested that kicking the caffeine habit would be good for him but giving up coffee was one step too far, even for love.

He grabbed a banana and wolfed it down, then looked for bread or a bagel. The closest thing he could find was a bag of rice cakes. 'Bleah,' he said.

He had to admit that he had lost a few pounds since Angie started living with him, but sometimes chili and burgers plagued him in his dreams.

A car horn squawked. 'Dammit,' Kahn shouted. Coffee splashed over the countertop as he transferred the hot brew into a travel mug, grabbed his shoulder holster and his jacket, and headed for the door, picking up another banana on the way.

He ran down the stairs and out the front door of the apartment building. Wagner's beat-up Cadillac sat across the parking lot, rumbling and spewing fumes – there was no way it was passing its next smog check.

'Geez Louise, Harlen, the neighbors are gonna kill me,' Kahn said as he jumped into the front seat.

As if on cue, Morris Goldberg, Kahn's next-door neighbor, appeared on his balcony. He was dressed in a plaid robe and clutched the morning newspaper. 'Hey! Hey, Mr. Horn Player. You could wake the dead you're so loud.' He shook the paper at them. 'I know who you are, Mr. Kahn.'

'Sorry about that, Mr. G,' Kahn called, and waved to the old man. 'I'll ask him not to honk his horn anymore.'

Harlen smiled. He stomped the gas and the car heaved forward. 'If I don't toot my own horn, who will?' he asked. 'Besides, I figured maybe you and Angie were, you know, occupied. I didn't want to come a-knockin' if the apartment was a-rockin'.'

'Classy.'

'Is that breakfast or lunch?' Harlen asked, jerking his thumb toward the banana.

'Breakfast. Damn. I forgot my coffee.'

'Don't drop the peel in my car. I have standards.'

Kahn laughed, and made a show of staring around the car's interior. Everything was dirty, dinged or dented. Crumpled fast-food sacks littered the back seat. The faded vinyl roof, an aftermarket add-on, was pulling loose. Harlen had taped it down with duct tape. Wires hung from beneath the dash, the ashtray overflowed, and the car smelled like a camel. The faded pin-up air freshener had been drained by foul odors years ago but still it hung from the rearview mirror.

Harlen took another drag on his cigarette and flicked it into the street. 'Did Wallace call you this morning?' He held his pack of cigarettes toward Kahn.

'No. What's up?' He took a cigarette and lit up.

'You know, you should either quit or man up and tell Angie you smoke. Then you can buy a pack of your own.'

'I'm quitting. How many do I bum from you in a day, four or five? I'll buy you a fucking pack, okay?'

'That's not the point, but whatever. Anyway, Phil said some guy named Zane Kowalski got splattered last night. A porn producer. They're bringing in boxes of his finest work. She thought you and I might do a few quick scans and see if we can find anyone of value.'

'Who are we looking for?'

'I don't know yet. I don't know if she knows. Who cares? Hey, speaking of porn, I met me a new woman last night. Sweet and naughty Monica.'

Kahn knew that as fabulous as this Monica might be this morning, she would soon be reduced to a name in Harlen's phone. Alison, Angelica, Beth, Cassandra, Cathy, Darlene, Debbie, Denise, Dolly – at the last count, the list went from A to Y skipping only Q and not quite reaching Z, but several letters repeated, especially D.

'Man, she is one crazy redhead. She could not keep her hands off this,' he said, gesturing up and down his body.

'What do you know about the porno guy?'

'Nothin'. I guess Wallace and her pal Sal are over there now.'

'Wallace didn't say anything about the dead guy?'

41

'She said he had his head beat in. And they found a ton of porn in the guy's pool-house.'

'Location?'

'By the pool.'

'No, dumbass. Not the pool-house. Where is the crime scene?'

Harlen laughed. 'Calm down. I was pulling your Richard. It's over on Laurel Canyon. What's the matter with you? Is he your porn supplier or something? I'm trying to tell you about Monica and you're going all detective on me.'

'Harlen, I don't really want to hear about another one of your sexual escapades right now.'

'O-kay,' he said, stretching out the word to suggest he wasn't happy being dressed down by his partner. 'Did Angie give you a wedgy or what?'

'Don't. I'm not in the mood. Let's not discuss Angie, either. I've got things on my mind.'

'Sounds like trouble in paradise. You want to tell me about it?'

'No. Not right now. Later.' Kahn didn't have to look at Harlen to know he was wearing his 'pissed' face. They had been partners now for seven years. It wasn't like they picked one another, it just happened. Once they were teamed up, they had become an effective team and close friends. They had

42

even been mistaken for brothers on more than one occasion – usually when they were out bar-hopping, so maybe the alcohol played a role. Still, it was an easy mistake to make. Both were pushing six foot two inches and both had blond hair, though Wagner's was starting to recede.

Despite Wagner's poor grooming, questionable morals and often one-dimensional conversation, there wasn't another detective on the squad Kahn would prefer to have by his side. Sure, things had changed a bit since Angie came along, but the guy had saved his life more than once. Kahn patted his jacket pocket to make sure the ring was still there. He had been carrying it around for two weeks and still hadn't asked her, but tonight he would do it. He had reservations at Davey Jones. A bouquet of roses would be on the table. Everything was set. But he hadn't told Harlen yet.

Harlen thought women were good for one thing, two if they could cook. To him, marriage was nothing but a mantrap created by a group of succubi demons who seduced unwitting mortal men and produced demonic offspring. Harlen would, to say the least, be pissed. Was it wrong that he was more worried about his partner's reaction than Angie's?

'So do you have any guesses on who the new guy will be?' Harlen said as he turned onto North Wilcox.

'I think Brooks plans on introducing him sometime this morning.' Kahn checked his watch against the clock on the bank.

'Yeah, but do you have any guesses who it might be? No one seems to know who it is. Usually with staff changes, there are all kinds of rumors.'

'Not a clue.'

'My guess is that it will be some Taco Paco. Lose one, get one.'

'Don't do that, man. It makes you sound like a racist.'

'Seriously. Siley's desperate to keep the racial balance. With Rodriguez gone, the chief needs to find another minority to move into the detective ranks. It sure won't be a white guy.'

'You've already been called on the carpet a few times for being, and I quote, "overzealous with suspects". If you get nailed for comments like that, you'll be scheduled for sensitivity training. That means you don't play nice with other cops. You get that tag in your file and the chances of getting a promotion go way down. I mean, way down. Virtually zero.'

'Phfft. I've gone as far as I'm going, Donny old boy. You know it and I know it. I've stepped on a few toes, bent a few beaks; I'm not PC. I just hope I can hold on to the rank I've got until I retire.'

'You never know what might happen. All you have to do is save the mayor's life or something like that and you'll be a lieutenant overnight. Besides, retirement is a long way off.'

'Or I could screw up one fucking report and end up getting demoted like Rodriguez. Seriously, if they can do that to a minority and no one raises a stink, I ain't got a prayer.'

'It wasn't only a report he screwed up. Porter should have gotten life. Instead he got off with minimum – eight years – because Rod messed up. The brass wasn't about to step in to protect his ass. Shit, they were worried about their own pensions. And anyway, he didn't get demoted. They moved him away from the fire.'

'Exactly. And how fast do you think you or I would get shuffled off to Bumfuck, Egypt?'

'Van Nuys isn't exactly Bumfuck, Egypt.'

'Pretty close. Okay, maybe not, but most people don't plan on screwing up. It just happens.' Harlen pulled to the curb. 'Breakfast?'

'I thought you were in a hurry to get to work.'

'We've got time. I could hear your stomach growling the minute you got in the car. Since you were carrying a banana and calling it breakfast, I'm guessing the little lady didn't whip you up anything substantial. What was it, oatmeal?'

Kahn stared out the front window.

45

'Worse than oatmeal?'

Kahn turned his head slightly and frowned.

'Aw, hell, even if she did make something, it would have been organic or healthy. Seriously, there's something wrong with serving a man eggplant and tofu omelet surprise. That's not man food. It doesn't stick to your ribs. Let's go into Sid's. I could use something myself. I was a little over-served last night in more ways than one.'

'I have to admit, I've had a taste for some pancakes and bacon since I woke up.'

'Yeah, I understand. Maybe it's something in the air, but I've had a craving for a Spanish omelet.'

'You're a funny man, Harlen.'

5

Reyes left the locker room feeling refreshed by a quick shower and a change of clothes. His shirt was wrinkled but wearable, and thanks to a few shots of Febreze, it smelled okay. He hurried to the interrogation room, arriving as the interpreter, Sylvia Howell, finished preparing Mrs. Cortez' statement.

Reyes looked it over and nodded. 'Okay, Mrs. Cortez,' he said in Spanish. 'Thank you.

46

If you would sign it here, you can go home.'

'*Gracias,*' she said. She signed the paper and moved swiftly, gathering her things, gesturing to Sara to pick up her drawings she had been working on.

'We called your husband,' Reyes said. 'But he said he couldn't come and pick you up. He apparently is having trouble with his car.'

'What?' She appeared confused.

Reyes repeated himself.

'No, no,' she said. 'We'll take the bus.'

'Not after the morning you two have had. I'll have an officer drive you home.'

'No, no, thank you. The bus is fine,' she said.

'We'll take you home,' Reyes repeated firmly. 'You go with Sylvia and she'll make sure you get a ride, won't you, Sylvia?'

'I will,' Sylvia said.

'*Adios,* Sara. *Adios,* Mrs. Cortez,' Reyes said. '*Gracias.*'

'*Adios,*' Mrs. Cortez said. '*Da nada.*'

Sara smiled, took her drawings and grasped her mother's hand. As she walked away, she turned and looked back. '*Adios,*' she said. It was faint but at least she no longer seemed to be as terrified as she had been a few hours ago.

Poor kid, Reyes thought. *I wonder how Nando would have reacted to that same situation. Damn. Nando's birthday present!* He had to get out at lunch and buy something.

47

He remembered the warning Pam had left on his answering machine: 'No guns. Nothing violent. Remember who you're buying a present for. Try to get something he likes, not something you like. For instance, he doesn't like soccer; he likes football. And don't be late. If you're late, don't bother coming at all. I'll be damned if you ruin his birthday again.' *She could at least have waited until I fucked up before she started bitching at me.*

Wallace stepped out of the adjacent break-room. She took a sip from her 'Support Our Troops' mug and made a face. 'At least Starbucks won't have to worry about competition from us.'

'If you put half and half and a ton of sugar in it, you hardly notice the coffee. It's an old Mexican secret called *café con leche*.' He waited for his partner to respond but she stared into her cup as if it were swamp-water. He moved on. 'Mrs. Cortez didn't give us much that we didn't already know. You want to read it?' He offered her the statement.

She waved it away. 'Just give me anything new. We've got that meeting in a few minutes.'

'Okay,' Reyes said. 'Well, the new stuff would be that Kowalski contacted Mrs. Cortez about two weeks ago and asked her not to come back until he called again. He did that yesterday and said she should resume the regular schedule starting today. When she

48

arrived, she found Kowalski lying dead on the floor and called nine-one-one, which, by the way, I suspect she was hesitant to do.'

'Why would she be hesitant?'

'She and her husband are illegal aliens. I got that out of her before Sylvia arrived to take her statement. I told her we weren't the INS but I couldn't promise anything regarding their status. And speaking of taking statements, that rule about using a certified translator is kind of stupid. I'm a native-born Mexican and I'm not allowed to interview a native-born Mexican in our native language.'

'You read the memo. All you have to do is attend the class and get certified and you can be a translator if that's what you want.'

'Great. So instead of using a Mexican-born citizen, we use a woman who was taught Spanish in L.A. public schools and at USC. *Muy bueno.*'

'Spoken like a true UCLA Bruin,' Wallace said. 'But you know why the rule is in place. Rodriguez and the Porter fiasco was the final straw. Before that, we had the beating of that rape suspect, A.C. Johnson, which some concerned citizen kindly videotaped. We also had the wounding of those two kids, neither of whom had a gun. That one will be hanging around in the courts for a few years – or until the LAPD settles. Too many mistakes, too close together. The Chief is reacting to the pressure he's getting from the media and

49

politicians.' She sipped her coffee.

'I understand all that, but we're talking about taking a statement here, not nailing some mob boss. It's a stupid rule and a waste of time and money.'

'We need a big win to lift the pressure,' she said. 'As for Mrs. Cortez, did she know why Kowalski didn't want her to come in for two weeks?'

'According to Sylvia,' he said, faking a cough, 'no. But that does explain the dust we found. She wasn't banging Kowalski. She wasn't even there.'

'So she says.'

'So you still think she was being black-mailed for sex?'

'All we know is that for some reason, Kowalski took a two-week break from having his house cleaned. That doesn't mean he was or wasn't banging her and/or blackmailing her. I'd say the possibility of her being se-duced by a threat of deportation is still a viable one.' Wallace checked her watch. 'It's nearly ten. The Captain wanted to see me before the meeting. I have to go. And a heads-up: Siley is feeling the pressure from above, as well, so unless I miss my guess, he's going to assume his General Patton persona.'

'Oh God,' Reyes said. 'Thanks for the warning. I'll try to keep a straight face.'

'I have to run.'

'Hey, Phil. I heard we're getting the new

guy today. Do you know who it is?'

She stared at him. 'You have a partner so it shouldn't affect you one way or another, right?' There was no emotion in her face or tone.

'I was just curious,' he said.

They started walking. 'The announcement is in about five minutes so we'll all know soon.' They turned into the cubicle area that the detectives called The Pit. Wallace stopped at the door to Captain Sileys office. 'See you in the meeting,' she said, then opened the door.

Reyes turned left and headed for his cubicle – third one on the left. He threw Mrs. Cortez' statement on top of his in-basket, then glanced at Siley's office where he could see Phil and the Captain most likely discussing the coming briefing. She was a good cop, but did she have to talk to him like he was a rookie? After six months of being her partner, he realized that was her style, but it didn't make it less annoying. Reyes dropped into his chair and rummaged through his desk drawers looking for something to eat. He found a can of toasted almonds. Not much of a breakfast but it would have to do. It sure wasn't as good as the two Stan's peanut butter and banana doughnuts he'd seen in the back of Donawald's car.

'Hey, Sal,' Emilio Albanese said, leaning over the cubicle wall. 'Did Phil say anything about my new guy?'

Reyes always thought that Albanese, with his raven-black hair and Roman features, should be on the cover of *GQ*. He wore expensive suits and a pearly white smile equally well. They had been partners for two days when Phil was sick and after Rodriguez had transferred. Every place they stopped, women made no attempt to hide the fact that they were staring. Albanese knew they were, of course, and was cocky about it, but never over-stepped the mark with the ladies. Some guys had all the luck.

'No,' Reyes said. 'She didn't say anything.' His cubicle neighbor was staring at the almonds. 'Want some?' he asked, offering him the can.

'Sure,' Albanese said, and poured a few into his hand. 'You should come down to my parents' restaurant. They serve a toasted almond tiramisu that is so good you'd be willing to give up sex to get a second helping.'

'Considering my recent history with women, that wouldn't be much of a sacrifice.'

Wagner stepped into Reyes' cubicle. 'I think you're trading a Mexican for a Mexican,' he said.

'What?' Albanese said. 'Oh. It's you. I should have known you'd have something brilliant to say.' He handed the can back to Reyes.

'What's that supposed to mean?' Wagner

said. 'I heard the new guy is a Mexican. Your old partner Rodriguez was a Mexican, wasn't he? That's all I'm saying.'

'Let's go,' Reyes said. 'It's time for the meeting.'

The detectives left The Pit and turned right past the break-room where Kahn was pouring himself a cup of coffee. He hurried to join them.

Albanese dropped back a step to check his reflection in the glass of interrogation room one.

Wagner and Kahn took seats together in the back row on the left. Reyes sat in the second row on the aisle. Ever since his first day on the job, when Wagner thought he was a street punk riffling through a cop's desk drawer and tried to cuff him, their relationship had been strained. Phil told him that's just how Wagner was, but the man had something to say about everything and much of it was ignorant shit.

Albanese stood at the back of the room near the door and sucked on his version of a cowboy's piece of straw, a ginger-flavored toothpick.

Captain Siley and Wallace walked in together and made for the front of the room. Wallace took a seat in the first row, center. Captain Siley stood opposite her, behind the podium. He was short, bald like a tonsured monk, and growing older by the

53

second. Phil said that since the heart attack forced him off the streets, he had lost his drive. Reyes knew that she'd covered for him on more than one occasion. Sometimes she seemed to be his only friend.

'Alright, men,' Siley said, 'the shit has hit the fan. We're being attacked on all fronts. You've all heard the old cliché that when the going gets tough...'

Wallace looked over her shoulder at Reyes. She rolled her eyes and turned back.

'...the tough get going. Well, it's time for us to get tough. You've all heard that Representative Juarez wants an investigation into our department's operating procedures – that there might be some major changes, maybe even having the detective division swallowed up by Robbery–Homicide.

'You all know about the murder last night. In and of itself, that would be no great shakes, but where it happened and the brutality of the attack was like pouring blood upon the water. The sharks smelled it. It's been on the radio almost before we had our first guy on the scene.

'So here's what we're going to do. All of the cases you are working on, put them on the back burner. Every detective in this squad is going to share this one and we are going to solve it as fast as possible. However, no matter how fast we go, we have to make sure every rule and regulation is followed. Cross the *T*'s. dot the *I*'s. Here's our motto for today,' he said, and picked up an index card. 'Less Starbucks, more Nike.'

'That's a crappy motto.' Wagner asked, 'What the hell does that even mean?'

'It means, quit sitting on your ass and get onto your feet,' Siley said. 'Deputy Chief Murray is promising the press results. I hate to make the old pot-licker look good, but if there is anyway you can figure out "whodunnit" before *CSI Miami* tonight, I'll buy the first round.'

'Yeah, like that'll happen. Hey, maybe we should watch *CSI* first to see how real police solve crimes,' Wagner said.

There was a smattering of laughs, and Reyes joined in. It was a joke throughout the division that DC Murray believed *CSI* was a reality show and couldn't figure out why his detectives didn't solve their cases in sixty minutes.

Even 'Dry-Siley' managed a smile. If there were two things Reyes and the others knew for certain about Siley, it was his lack of a sense of humor and his dislike of Deputy Chief Murray, whom he said had been promoted because of who he knew, not what he knew.

'Sorry to say, we have no time to gather around the boob tube so we'll have to fake it,' Siley said. 'Wallace is the lead investigator on this one. She's going to brief you and then give each team their assignment. Any questions?'

'Yeah. I have one,' Albanese said. 'Where's my partner? Wasn't that supposed to happen today?'

'The new guy was supposed to be here at ten,' Siley said. 'Ray is waiting downstairs.' He shrugged. 'I'm sure they'll be here any minute.'

'Good Lord, Ray is the welcome wagon?' Wagner said.

'Give it a rest,' Siley said. 'Ray Brooks has forgotten more about being a cop than you'll ever know. Phil, you ready?'

'Yes,' she said, and stepped up to the podium. 'Some time last night, between midnight and two, Zane Kowalski was beaten to death in his house on Laurel Canyon Road up in the old section of the Hills. If his name sounds vaguely familiar it's because he was the producer of the movie, *The Scarlet Mays Affair*. He was accused of statutory rape by the teenage star. She and her mother left the state and headed for New York. Pretty good guess that she was paid off. The case died but that was the last family entertainment Kowalski made. He apparently moved into porn. We discovered a cache of movies and a mini-production-center at Kowalski's house.'

Reyes couldn't help looking at Wagner, who sat with his feet on the back of the chair in front, a smirk across his face.

'Might have been a robbery gone bad,' Wallace continued. 'There appeared to be a few things missing...'

Reyes listened as Wallace laid out the rest of the background. 'No witnesses. The neighbors didn't hear a thing.

'We need someone to run through some of the newer porn flicks we've recovered and see if we can recognize any of the stars,' Wallace said. 'It's a long shot but I'm sure Wagner and Kahn won't mind checking them out.'

'It's going to be hard,' Wagner said, then paused, 'but somebody's got to do it.'

Wallace ignored him and went on. 'Kowalski was slaughtered, his face literally removed by the beating he took. The neighbors are afraid that a psycho is on the loose. The media are going to fuel that fear if they haven't already. I wouldn't be surprised to see a video of the damned murder scene on the Internet.'

'Not on MyFace,' Wagner quipped.

'To speed along our own investigation,' Wallace said, 'each team will be given a specific part to focus on. We can be in three or four places at once. Brooks will be coordinating things here and keep you all up to date as things unfold.'

'Speaking of Brooks, where the hell is he?' Albanese asked. 'Shouldn't my partner be attending this meeting?'

'I told you, ten o'clock,' Siley said. He

looked at the clock on the wall. It was now ten-eighteen. 'I don't know where in the hell they are.'

'Maybe he stopped for a siesta,' Wagner said.

Reyes shook his head. 'Fuck your pasty white ass, Wagner.'

'Kowalski had a junior business partner by the name of Trey Brightman,' Wallace said. 'He's already talked to the D.A. By the way, he's a former porn star himself. His stage name was Johnny Pounder. I think both of his names may be misnomers if you get my drift.'

The unexpected humor from Wallace caught the room off guard. Reyes smiled.

'Brightman gave us two leads. He said that Kowalski had argued with a guy named Denver Collins the night he was killed. Collins lives out in Calabasas. His sheet includes assault and battery. He beat up his girlfriend some time back although he's been clean since. But here's a stunner – Collins is also a movie producer.'

'Or it could be someone whacking porn barons,' Wagner said.

'We'll bear that in mind, Harlen,' said Wallace. 'But at the moment we only have one body. Brightman also told us that Kowalski was close to a girl named Sadie Monaghan – one of his stars. He gave us her address but Sadie wasn't home so there are uniforms at the house waiting for her. Until we talk to her, she remains a person of interest.'

'If she's hot, then she's definitely a person of interest,' Wagner said. 'I volunteer to check her out.'

'Can't you shut the hell up for five minutes?' Reyes said. 'These meetings would take half as long if you didn't have to share your wit and wisdom all the time.'

'What crawled up your ass and died?' Wagner said.

'Guys,' Siley said rising slightly from his chair, 'can the comments.'

Wallace pushed on. 'The name of the victim isn't being released until we find the next of kin. Unfortunately, that may be tough. Brightman said he thought Kowalski's mom might be alive but he didn't know that for sure. He had no idea if she lives in the area, what her name is or, like I said, even if she's alive.'

'Does this Brightman guy have an alibi?' Kahn asked, but before Wallace could answer, the sound of shouting in the squadroom disrupted the briefing.

'What the hell is that?' Captain Siley asked, turning in his chair to locate the source of the noise.

Albanese was first out of the door and Reyes followed him back into the squadroom.

'Well, I'll be damned,' Emilio said. A petite

59

blonde, looking disheveled, the jacket sleeve of her pinstriped suit torn, was manhandling a ratty-looking thug past the meeting room. The cuffed man wore a sleeveless 'wife-beater' T-shirt that revealed muscular arms covered with tattoos promising death and destruction to everyone.

'Morning, boys,' she said, a slight strain in her voice. 'Booking's down the hall, I assume?'

The squad momentarily froze, Reyes more than anyone. Captain Siley pushed his way through until he stood in front of his squad. 'Wagner, put your eyes back into their sockets. Albanese, give your new partner a hand. Guys, this is Joanne Coombs, the department's new detective.'

Albanese instantly stepped from the pack. 'Hi. I'm Emilio Albanese,' he said as he grabbed the right arm of the cuffed man. 'Come on, I'll help you take your collar to booking.'

'Thanks,' she said. 'I've been away for a while. I wouldn't want to get turned around in here.'

She smiled at the rest of the squad. 'Hi, guys. Hi, Sal.'

Reyes nodded, his expression tight. Then he turned to Wallace, who shrugged.

'I'll give you all your assignments in a minute,' Wallace said. 'Come by and see me when you're ready to roll.'

'We'll be right back,' said Albanese. He and Coombs pushed through the double doors at the end of the detective's hallway and headed for booking.

Ray Brooks casually joined the group. 'Is she here yet?'

'Yes, she's here,' the Captain said. 'Where the hell have you been? You were supposed to escort her in.'

Brooks rubbed his stomach. 'When ya gotta go, ya gotta go.' He took a pack of Rolaids from his pocket and popped a couple into his mouth.

'Shit,' Siley said. 'Give me some of those. It's going to be a long, damned day.'

6

Reyes sat quietly at his desk, staring at a blank computer screen but seeing his past. It was almost five years ago now that he and Coombs had been assigned to Wilshire. They ran together. They patrolled together. They shared their thoughts. They talked about their dreams and hopes for nine hours a day, four days a week.

His dream was to finish his degree in Psychology at UCLA. She had majored in Criminal Justice and hoped to work her way up the ranks of the force. He was trying to save a marriage he never wanted. She didn't want to get married until her career was on solid footing. Both liked kids but wondered if being a cop would allow them time to be good parents. His first assignment was Robbery; hers was Juvenile Crime. A rash of teen break-ins prompted their commander to team up members from both divisions to work together and try to end the crime wave.

They had been on patrol when a call came in reporting suspicious activity behind a Chinese restaurant known as the Wok 'n' Roll. A suspected drug deal. It was a quiet night, around nine. They entered an alley behind the restaurant but found nothing. But as they approached a dumpster, they heard a noise. Reyes and Coombs drew their weapons and crept closer. They reached the stinking steel container, nodded to one another, and then rose above the edge with the guns pointed toward the fly-covered debris inside.

Expecting a young thug hiding from the cops, they found instead twin babies, quite alive. They each took one child and carried it back to their squad car, gently brushing off the fried rice and duck sauce. A small crowd gathered. The moment became Disneyesque. A blanket and a towel were offered by strangers to keep the little ones warm. A mother gave two bottles of formula from her own diaper bag. As the ambulance headed for the hospital with two healthy little ones wrapped warmly inside, Coombs kissed Reyes.

'I think I love you, Salvador,' she said.

Reyes struggled for the right response, a hundred things going through his mind at once: his wife Pam waiting at home, the bright blue of Joanne's eyes, the strictures of his faith on divorce, the soft touch of Joanne's lips on his...

The noisy exchanges between the other detectives bubbled over the wall of his cubicle, chasing away the memory. Reyes couldn't remember what he'd said back to Coombs. He only knew he had stumbled over his words and they were the wrong ones.

A week later Pam told him she was pregnant, and Coombs was selected for the FBI Academy at Quantico. She accepted instantly and left without saying goodbye. He remembered feeling hurt that she just disappeared from his life, but he soon came to realize that Joanne did what she had to do for both of their sakes.

'You two,' Wallace said to Wagner and Kahn, 'get to talk to the other porn producer in this melodrama, Denver Collins.'

'I thought we were going to check out the film you brought in from Kowalski's,' Wagner asked. 'I even have a bag of microwave popcorn in my desk.'

'Change of plan. We're giving that job to Brooks. He's going to do it while he co-ordinates our efforts from here,' she said. 'Sorry. I know you were looking forward to it. Who knows? Maybe this Collins guy will give you a free sample.'

'Watching stuff like that could kill Brooks,' Wagner said. 'I think you should reconsider.'

Wallace ignored him. 'Here,' she said, handing Wagner a manila folder. 'Read Collins' file. He's an interesting piece of work.'

Wagner flipped open the folder. Denver Collins' picture was stapled in the upper left-hand corner. 'Holy shit. He looks like that bat boy from the *National Enquirer,* only all grown up,' he said.

The picture showed a man with a slender face, long pointed nose and prominent ears.

'The sheriff said he has a man stationed outside of Collins' place. He'll be your back-up if you need a hand.'

'Okay,' Kahn said. 'You ready, Harlen?'

'I was born ready,' he said. 'But I can't believe I have to go see this bat boy instead of ogling some young nubiles.'

Wagner and Kahn headed for the back door of the station. Coombs and Albanese took their place in Wallace's cubicle.

'Welcome to the squad,' Wallace said, offering her hand to Coombs. 'I'm Philippa Wallace.'

'Thanks,' Coombs said. 'I'm Joanne

Coombs, but you already knew that, I guess. Anyway, it's nice to meet you. You had a rep when I used to work in Juvenile.'

Wallace gave her a puzzled look. 'A rep? I hope it was a good one.'

'Oh yeah, it was.' Coombs smiled.

Wallace nodded. 'I need you two to head over to the scene and check around the neighborhood. Nobody answered the door at a couple of the places, including the house that's directly behind Kowalski's. They might be interesting to talk to. The pool-house where he had all of his editing equipment was a few feet from their fence. Maybe they saw something.' She shrugged. 'You know the drill.' She handed a sheet of paper to Albanese. 'Here's who we talked to and the addresses of the houses where no one was home, Any questions?'

Coombs looked at Albanese. 'I don't think so. But before we go, Emilio's going to show me my desk, and then take me to get a weapon issued.'

'You have your own weapon?' Wallace asked.

'Yes, I do, but Emilio said it was SOP to have both.'

'I'm not sure we have a standard operating procedure for anything,' Wallace said.

'Kidding. Yeah, that's sort of how things are done around here. I have two, just in case.'

'Let's go get you fixed up,' Albanese said.

'The armory is back down the hall again. It's actually Sergeant Roberts locked cabinet but armory sounds more impressive. Come on, I'll give you the nickel tour.'

Wallace walked over to her partner's work space. 'Sal?'

'Yeah?'

'You okay?'

'Sure. Why wouldn't I be?'

'I don't know. I heard that you and Coombs used to be, well, kind of...'

'It was a long time ago. I'm fine.'

Wallace picked up the silver-framed picture of Fernando and looked at it. 'He looks like you.'

'Yeah. He and my coffeemaker are the only two good things I got out of that marriage.'

Wallace smiled. 'You ready to roll?'

'You bet, partner. What straw did we draw?'

'The girlfriend. Sadie Monaghan finally came home.'

7

Reyes turned east off of the I-5 onto the Imperial Highway heading toward Sadie Monaghan's apartment in La Mirada. He slowed as he eased the squad car past an accident – a Taurus with a kink in the bonnet and a red SUV. He waved to the cop directing traffic. 'Its kind of sad that the closest thing to a relative we can find for Kowalski is a girlfriend.'

'I suppose it is,' Wallace said. 'Turn right up here at Cordova. It's couple a hundred yards on the left. Cornfield Estate it's called.'

'Cornfield? Must have been a farm way back when, huh?'

'No, that's a guy's last name. This apartment complex and the park we passed were the estate of Augie Cornfield. He used to be a big shot in the early days of Hollywood.'

'I never heard of him. Did he make any big movies?'

'No. He made a lot, though. Then some young actress died at one of his wild parties. They said she had been sexually brutalized. Cornfield went into his garage, started the car and killed himself.'

'Interesting,' Reyes said.

'Rumors sprung up that someone killed Cornfield but no one was ever arrested for it.'

Reyes parked the car. 'Shall we go talk to the girlfriend?'

'Let's do it,' Wallace replied. As she shut the car door, she spotted a tall black cop standing outside the lobby door, shielding his eyes from the sun. 'Hey, Sal,' she said. 'It's Tibor Martin. Remember him?'

'He's the one who keeps finding reasons to take breaks, right?'

67

'That's our man.'

'Hey, guys. How you doing?' said Martin as they approached. 'The party is in thirteen G. My partner is up there with the Monaghan woman.'

'Thanks,' Wallace said. 'Is Monaghan in good shape emotionally?'

'Lots of crying,' Martin said. 'That's why I came down here.'

'Coward,' Reyes said. He winked.

They waved their badges at the concierge. She nodded and returned to her work. They took the elevator to the thirteenth floor Reyes knocked on 13G. Officer Tina Lantz opened the door.

'Hi,' she said. 'Miss Monaghan is in the parlor.' She jerked her thumb toward the front room. 'Do you want me in there while you question her?'

'Yeah. This shouldn't take long,' Wallace said. Her eyes scanned the room. 'This is a pretty fancy place.'

'She lives well,' Lantz said. 'This way.'

Lantz led them toward the parlor. A thin blonde woman sat quietly on a zebra-skin sofa that probably cost the same as Wallace's monthly mortgage payment. The room had one primary red wall. The other walls were pink with red or white accents. A white grand piano served as a photo display stand. Wallace stared momentarily at a white rolltop desk. Reyes nodded and wandered toward it.

'Miss Monaghan?' Wallace asked.

Sadie raised her head. Her hair was messed, her mascara streaked down her cheeks from bloodshot eyes. The ashtray was half-full of lipstick-stained cigarette butts and there was an empty glass in front of her. 'Yes?' she said, seemingly barely able to force a single word from her lips.

Wallace introduced Reyes and herself. 'Miss Monaghan. I can see this is a rough time for you but it is essential that I ask you a few questions. Do you think you're up to that?'

Monaghan sobbed. 'Yes. Maybe if I could have another small drink first.'

'Sure,' Wallace asked.

'I'll get it,' Lantz said. She winked at Wallace and shook the glass at her as she walked by, suggesting that the drink wasn't the first.

'Thank you. You're so nice,' Monaghan said. 'For a police officer, I mean.'

'You're welcome,' Lantz said. 'I think.'

When Lantz returned with a glass full of something brown, Monaghan took a few sips. 'Ah. That's better,' she said. 'Rum and Coke always remind me of Jamaica.' She lit a cigarette. Her body trembled as she exhaled. 'You know, Officer Lantz, if you ever decide to quit being a cop, you could get a job as a bartender. You mix a mean drink.' She took another sip. 'What do you want to know, um...?'

69

'Detective Wallace,' she said, introducing herself a second time. 'And that's Detective Reyes over there.' She gestured across the room, where Reyes was making a show of looking out the window. 'First things first. Could you tell me where you were last night Around midnight?'

'Ab-so-lutely. Zane and I were at a party at um ... Farmighetti's.'

'How long were you at the party?' asked Wallace.

Sadie dropped her eyes. 'Zane was pretty drunk. We left before midnight because we got to his house somewhere around, you know, midnight. Maybe a little after. I'm not one hundred per cent sure of the time.'

'Did Mr. Kowalski drink a lot?'

'He'd had a few beers and some martinis...'

'I mean, did he drink often? On a regular basis?'

'Oh. Sure. I mean, the man liked to party and that always included drinking. He had a ... um ... a bottle of every kind of booze they make. And he bought only the good stuff, too.'

Wallace thought back to the crime scene and the loaded bar. Something about it had bothered her then and now was back to bug her again.

'So, after you brought him home, what happened? Did you go inside for a drink?'

'No. No drinks. I think. I mean, I think nothing happened. We weren't ... um ... we weren't really seeing each other anymore. But!' She took a gulp. 'But we were still friends. And ... we still had a business relationship. I told him I had to get going because I had appointments in the morning. He said he was going to have a nightcap and go to bed. I kissed him good-night – you know, just friendly like, because we were still friends – did I tell you that? Well, anyway, then I got in my car and left. That was...' she sighed '...the last time I saw him.'

'So you two had split up?'

'Ladies don't hang onto Zane too long.'

'Why is that?'

'Well.' She shook her head. Let's say that ... well ... there is too much to choose from. You know? It's like a buffet. Lots and lots to choose from.' She lifted her glass in a half-assed salute.

'I see,' Wallace said. 'Can you tell me what kind of appointments you had scheduled for today?'

'Well, my first that was for, um, a manicure. That was at nine. I was scheduled to have my hair styled at ten-thirty. Let's see, after that I was ... I was meeting a business associate for lunch. At one. I was halfway through getting my nails done when Trey called on my cell and told me...'

'Mr. Brightman?'

71

'Yes. He called and said...' She hesitated again. Tears were welling up. 'I can't remember exactly. I just remember hearing–' she took a few quick breaths '–that Zane was dead.'

'And that news hit you hard, did it?' asked Wallace.

Reyes flashed her a look, as if to say *go easy on her*. Wallace shook her head.

'It sure did,' said Sadie. 'You know,' she exhaled, 'I ran away from home when I was fifteen. I came here because I thought I could become a star.'

'Who didn't?' Lantz mumbled.

'What?' Sadie asked, with a hint of anger. 'What did you say?'

'Nothing,' Wallace said. 'Go on.'

Sadie spoke more firmly now. 'I met Zane the second night I was in town. He was amazing. He took me home. Gave me a room. Fed me.' She held up her empty glass. 'Oh my. It's empty. Ms. Lantz, would you mind?'

Lantz looked at Wallace.

Reluctantly, Wallace said, 'One more, but I'd like you to stay focused here, Ms. Monaghan.'

'Oh, sure. Where was I?'

'When you first came to town...'

'Right. Well. Zane got me gigs. Dancing in clubs. Some modeling. It was mostly lingerie but, you know, famous models still strut for Victoria, and that's no secret.' She laughed at her play on words.

'Ms. Monaghan,' Wallace said. 'Focus.'

Sadie dabbed the tears from her eyes. 'Back home, I had trouble finding a job of any kind because of my age. Zane got me work right away. I wasn't getting rich but it was better than selling hamburgers at some drive-through.' She sobbed. 'I probably would have been on the streets if not for him. Zane put me in my first film.' Sadie looked at Lantz. 'Could you hurry that drink along, please?'

Lantz handed the drink to Sadie, who sipped it, then lit another cigarette, exhaled, and pushed on.

'I was a little hesitant to make the movie, because, well, you know.' She took another sip of her rum and Coke, spilling a few drops from the edge of her lips. She took the lime wedge that was clinging to the rim, squeezed it then dropped it back into the glass. 'It was an adult film and Zane and I were, um, like a couple. He said actors have to kiss and stuff but it's all for the camera. It's not real. It's acting. After the first movie, it was easier but we had to be careful because I was still ... you know ... a little young. Zane gave me a lot, but do you know what his best gift was? He made me a star.'

'Uh-huh. You said you ran away from home. Where was home?' Wallace asked.

'Coffee City, Texas,' she said. 'Most of my family is still there. And don't you worry. I call my mama all the time now. Everything is cool between us.'

'Does she know what you do for a living?'

'Of course,' Sadie said. 'I'm a secretary.' She smiled, her bright white teeth shining between magenta-colored lips. 'Mama has never once complained about the money I send her.'

'Did Mr. Kowalski ever mention his mother?'

'His mother?' Sadie frowned. 'I don't think he ever did. Why?'

'With you and your mom having such a close relationship, I'm surprised you asked. I thought his family might like to know that he's dead. Someone said they thought his mom was around somewhere. We thought you might know how to contact her.'

Sadie started sobbing. 'I feel for his mother but,' she took a deep breath, 'I don't know ... what I'm ... going to do.'

'Do?' Wallace asked. 'Do about what?'

Sadie took another deep breath and choked out, 'We were supposed to start filming a new movie tomorrow.' And then the weeping started in earnest. Lantz offered her the tissue box.

Wallace frowned. She waited but Sadie continued to cry like a jilted schoolgirl. 'I guess that's enough for now,' she said. 'I assume you're going to be around town, right?'

'Unless we sign to do an on-location picture, I plan on being here,' she said, her composure returning ever so slightly.

'You should plan on being here for the next forty-eight hours, even if you do sign up for an on-location shoot,' Wallace said. She handed one of her contact cards to Sadie. 'If you feel the need to get out of town, you call me first.'

'Why? You don't think I killed Zane, do you? Seriously, that would be preposterous. I couldn't have hurt him.'

'It's a crummy job having to suspect people of murder,' Wallace said. 'But someone has to do it until folks stop killing each other.'

Sadie fanned herself with a magazine. 'Is that all? I feel woozy. I need to lie down.'

Wallace signaled to Officer Lantz. 'Take Ms. Monaghan to her bedroom. Have her call a friend or her agent or somebody, then let her lie down. You can cut out after that.'

'Will do,' Officer Lantz said. She took Sadie by the arm and helped her stand. The young woman's thin tanned legs were unsteady. After Lantz shut the bedroom door, Wallace turned to Reyes.

'Find anything?' she asked.

'Not much,' Reyes said. 'Look at this, though. I found a movie script over on the desk. I'm guessing it's the one they were supposed to start shooting tomorrow.' He handed the script to Wallace. 'It doesn't have much of a plot, but check out the title. Ironic, eh?'

Wallace took the script – *Headbangers: A Zane Kowalski Film.* 'Yeah,' she said. 'That is kind of weird.' She threw the script onto the coffee table.

When they leached the car. Wallace looked at Reyes and said, 'I will say this for Kowalski. He recognized talent when he saw it.'

'I don't follow.' Reyes started the car. 'You think Monaghan has potential?'

'She just put on an acting clinic for us. She brought up those crocodile tears on command.'

'That was an act?' Reyes said. 'Impressive.'

'Did you hear her say she got the call halfway through getting her nails done?'

'Yeah.'

'It's been three or four hours and she still is so distraught she can hardly talk, but she wasn't so shook up immediately after she got the call.'

'Why do you say that?'

'She stayed long enough to get her nails finished.'

Reyes waved goodbye to Martin and backed the car from the parking space.

'Sadie is a tough cookie,' Wallace said. 'I doubt that she would shed tears if someone microwaved her puppy. And don't forget, she and Kowalski were no longer lovers. I can't believe the death of an ex-boyfriend would bring on such an emotional outburst.'

'Why the show then?' Reyes asked.

'My guess is that she's hiding something. She's looking for sympathy.'

'You think she might have done it?'

'I sure as hell ain't crossing her off the list.'

8

'I could get comfortable with the new broad,' Wagner said. 'She has a nice ass and there was no VPL. You know what that means, right?'

Kahn grunted a negative. Traffic on the 101 was heavy. He checked his blind spot and eased the car over to take the Mulholland Drive exit.

'No visible panty line. She's going commando.' Wagner whistled.

'She's hot, alright,' Kahn said as he turned onto the slip road. 'I'd be careful, though. She strikes me as the kind who would tear off your ankles if you tried anything. That guy she dragged in was bigger than you.'

'I still say that she'd be a good partner.'

'Looking to replace me? Because if you are, I can quit wearing underwear if that will help.'

'Thanks for that image. Shit. No, partner, I'm just saying that, you know, in case you ever screw up a report or something that would take you off the streets, I'd consider Coombs as your replacement.'

'You would, huh? Decent of you.'

'I bet she can do things you can't,' Wagner said. 'Things they don't teach at the Academy. Either way, she sure is easier on the eyes.' He rolled down the window and flipped his cigarette butt to the curb. 'Turn right. Hey, on the way out, how about we stop at the Sagebrush Cantina? Man, I love their steak tacos. They give me gas, though.' He rubbed his stomach.

'I know,' said Kahn.

Mulholland twisted around, joined Old Topanga Canyon Road, and then split again. The sheriff's cruiser was waiting for them. Kahn pulled up alongside. Wagner rolled the window down.

'Hi. Kahn and Wagner. Hollywood Precinct. This Collins' place?' Wagner asked, pointing to the large white house that squatted behind a fence.

'Yup. I'll wait here until you come out,' the deputy said.

'Thanks for the cover,' Wagner said, and rolled up the window. A wrought-iron gate funneled guests onto a heart-shaped driveway. In the center of the heart was a gaudy fountain in which marble nymphs frolicked with a centaur. The house was a mock-gothic horror, designed by someone with too much money and not enough taste.

'Holy shit, if this place isn't ugly as sin, I don't know what is,' Wagner said as he slammed the car door.

'It sure isn't going to be mistaken for a *Playboy* mansion,' Kahn said as he rang the bell. It played the theme to *Chorus Line.* 'This place looks like it was designed by Siegfried and Roy.'

The heavy door swung open. The house might not have lived up to *Playboy* standards, but the woman standing in front of them more than made up for it. She was young – a blue-eyed, bleached blonde – in a French-maid uniform. Only if this maid bent over to dust the floor, it would be indecent – the dress came to the tops of her thighs. Wagner stared.

'I'm Detective Kahn. The guy drooling on himself is Detective Wagner. We're here to see Denver Collins.'

'Come in,' she said, opening the door further and gesturing for them to step inside. 'If you wait here in the foyer, I'll announce you.'

'How about if we follow along now?' Kahn said. 'We're kind of in a hurry. Besides, Mr. Collins is expecting us.'

'Besides that, I'll enjoy watching you walk,' Wagner said. 'What did you say your name was?'

'It's Dawn.'

'How about if we have breakfast tomorrow? I can be up – at dawn.'

She shook her head. 'This way,' she said. She walked like she was on a runway. They crossed through the front room. The walls were covered with photos of nude and semi-nude women. The furniture looked like it belonged to a sheik – overstuffed furniture with large pillows, gold brocade on the drapes.

They entered another hallway, illuminated by the natural ambient light streaming through a number of skylights, and passed an indoor solarium filled with plants and butterflies. Kahn glanced at the steamy display of nature inside, but Wagner focused on the maid's behind. She stopped directly under one of the skylights and knocked on a door to her left.

'Come,' a man's voice said from the other side. It was Californian with a hint of a patrician drawl.

Dawn opened the door but kept one hand on the knob, the other on the frame. 'Mr. Collins, the police are here. They want to speak with you. They said you were expecting them.'

'Oh yes.' came the voice from inside the room. 'I was told they might be stopping by. Tell them to come in if they wish but I'm right in the middle of this edit. They'll have to wait a second.'

The maid stepped aside. 'He'll be right with you. You can have a seat in the back of the film room if you wish.'

'Thanks,' Kahn said. He tugged Wagner's arm. 'Come on, Romeo.'

The detectives stepped into a dimly lit studio. Dominating the room were five rows of theater seating, seven seats wide, facing a curtained area, behind which Kahn guessed there was a screen. Over the far side of the room, through an open pair of double doors, was a slight man in his forties, wearing glasses. He was wearing some kind of hat. The muffled sounds of two people having sex reached Kahn's ears.

Dawn leaned forward and whispered. 'Maybe Mr. Collins will let you see my movie. Ask him for *Dawn at Midnight.*' She smiled, winked at Wagner and left the room, closing the door behind her.

Both men remained standing at the back of the studio for a moment, then Kahn made his way toward Collins' anteroom. As he came closer, and his eyes became used to the light, he realized that the hat was actually a bandage. A shock of pale hair sat above it. The man looked like Andy Warhol.

The source of the sounds was on a wide screen that Denver Collins was watching intently, where a redhead handcuffed to a jail-cell door was performing oral sex on a man dressed as a cop. A man stood behind her wearing a judge's robes. Wagner was wide-eyed beside Kahn as the judge dropped the robe and mounted the woman from behind. Soon the three performers had fallen into a rhythm.

'That's a talent,' Wagner muttered.

'Denver Collins?' Kahn asked.

'Denver Collins the second,' the man said. 'But I thought we had agreed that you would be quiet until I finished this edit. Or was that two other cops I invited into my home?'

'That must have been two other guys because these two cops are going to drag your ass downtown right now if you don't hit Pause,' Kahn said.

Wagner looked at his partner with a silent pleading to let the film run to its climax.

Kahn shook his head. 'Mr. Collins?'

'Sorry, boys, but isn't she great?' he asked, pointing to the woman in the video. 'That's my girl, Velma.'

'Velma Vixen? I thought I recognized the tits,' said Wagner, leaning closer to get a better look.

'The one and only,' Collins said.

'It's been a few years,' said Wagner, 'but I used to be a fan.'

Collins frowned. 'Well, she's no ingénue, but she's no grandmother, either.'

'Mr. Collins,' Kahn said. He drew his finger across his throat.

Collins sighed. 'Okay, I get it. Good cop,

horny cop.' He clicked the pause switch, then spun in his chair to face them.

'A little light, please,' Kahn said.

Collins spun back toward the console and turned a dial. The room lights came up. 'How's that? Everything to your liking now?'

'That'll do just fine,' Kahn said. 'I assume the sheriff told you why we wanted to talk to you?'

'Oh yes,' he said, and turned back to look up at the two officers. 'Sheriff John Stone. I asked him if he knew that his name was famous in song. He said he knew and, here I quote, "he didn't give a flying fuck".'

'We're investigating the murder of Zane Kowalski,' Kahn said.

'Ah, the late, unlamented Zane Kowalski. The way the news is portraying him you'd think he was another Spielberg. The reality is that he was a no-talent hack who tried...' Collins stopped midsentence.

'Tried what?' Kahn asked.

'Nothing, really.' Collins scrunched his face. 'He tried his hand at things he knew nothing about. You know, he wandered into deep water. Drink, officers?'

'Yeah,' Wagner said. 'I'll have a whiskey and water.'

'And you?' he asked Kahn.

'No, just a few answers,' Kahn said. 'We're not here to socialize.' He frowned at Wagner. 'You want to tell us where you were around midnight last night, Mr. Collins? Say between midnight and two?'

'One moment,' Collins said. He rolled his chair back to the wall, reached up and pushed a call button on the intercom.

'Yes, Mister Collins?'

The kind of voice you'd pay three ninety-nine a minute to talk with, Kahn thought.

'Would you bring us a whiskey and water and a glass of red wine for me, please?'

'On its way,' the voice lilted back.

'Now, you wanted to know where I was. That is an easy one,' Collins said. 'I was in the St. Regis Clinic until this morning.' He patted the bandage on his head. 'Nearly concussed.'

'How did you get "nearly concussed"?' Wagner asked.

'I think you know the answer,' Collins said, a grin spreading across his narrow face. His eyebrows twitched.

'You ran into a door?' Kahn asked.

'I fell. Same thing.'

There was a sound of a door opening and Kahn turned to see Dawn sashaying across the theater room carrying a tray with two drinks.

She paused for an instant until Collins pointed at Wagner. She handed him the whiskey and water, then turned and placed the wine on the work table next to Collins. 'Nothing for you?' she asked Kahn.

'Thanks, no.'

Dawn left the room. Collins picked up his glass, raised it and said, '*Salut.*' He took a sip. 'Ah, that is good stuff. Nineteen eighty-nine Silver Oak Cabernet Sauvignon. Sonoma Valley. Have you tried it?'

'What I drink comes in cans and has a "born on" date,' Kahn said. 'Let's go back to Mr. Kowalski. I know you were in the same business? Were you friends, as well?'

'The same business?' Collins waved a hand. 'We weren't remotely in the same *business.* Kowalski's films were garage-made garbage. Tacky, poor quality, questionable talent.'

'So you two weren't in competition?' asked Kahn.

Collins looked him dead in the eye. 'He was no threat to me, if that's what you mean.'

Kahn nodded, then made a show of consulting his notebook. 'Mr. Collins, we have a witness who told us that you and the deceased argued recently. Care to explain that?'

'Oh please. A witness?'

'Collins' partner, Trey Brightman.'

Collins gave a bitter laugh. 'Brightman, huh? That guy should have stuck to the horizontal stuff. Well-endowed below the waist, but that's about it. He thinks he's a director now.'

'And he isn't?'

'Don't make me laugh.'

'Mr. Collins,' Kahn persisted, 'did you

have an argument?'

Collins smiled. 'That was nothing. I found out Kowalski approached my distributor looking for a deal. The thought was laughable, but still, as the song says, "he was messin' where he shouldn't have been messin'". If you can't get your films to the end users, you aren't in this business very long.'

'And?' asked Kahn.

'I had to put a stop to it, of course, but Kowalski wouldn't return my calls. As luck would have it, I ran into him last night and told him how I felt about his tactics. It was over and done before I left for home.'

'So, he just said, "Okay, fine" and that was that?'

Wagner finished his drink, wiped his lips with his knuckle, and reached for his cigarettes. 'Mind if I smoke?'

'Feel free,' Collins said. 'And yes, that was that. Like I said, he was an amateur I had to let him know how one conducts business properly. Once I explained it, he decided to back off.'

'This was last night?'

'Yes. I was having dinner out and ran into him and one of his girls.'

'Where and when did this chance encounter take place?'

'Farmighetti's. I don't know the exact time but it was probably somewhere around nine or ten.'

'Can you think of anyone who might want to kill Mr. Kowalski?' Kahn asked.

'Well, there's me, of course,' Collins said, a wide grin on his face. 'But I didn't do it. I would suspect that any of the ladies he featured in his movies might want to kill him for ruining their careers. Maybe that blonde chick he was with last night. Other than that, I hardly knew the man, so I'm afraid I can't help you.'

'Do you know who this blonde chick was?'

'I've seen her around. I think someone said she was dating Kowalski. I'm not sure, though.'

Kahn pulled out a card. 'If you think of anything that might help us, you give me a call.'

'Oh, you know I will,' Collins said. 'Can't have someone going around killing producers now, can we? He might actually get one the next time.'

Wagner's cell phone rang. 'Excuse me,' he said, and stepped into the hall.

'Thanks for your time,' Kahn said. 'We'll show ourselves out.'

'Would you do me a small favor, officer?' Collins asked. He dipped his finger into his wine, dabbed it behind his ears, and then ran his fingertip around the lip of his wineglass.

'What is it?'

'Tell the sheriff his watchdog can go home. His little deputy has been sitting in his squad car outside my gate. It gives the neighborhood a bad name.'

Kahn nodded and joined Wagner in the hall where he was talking with Dawn. 'Here's my card,' he was saying. 'Call me.'

Dawn smiled briefly then showed the two detectives out.

'Losing your touch?' Kahn asked.

'Not at all. I'm just not a morning person. Get it?'

Kahn laughed. 'Not bad. Was that call anything?'

'Yeah. They got a match on the fingerprints at the crime scene. A two-time loser named Henry "Big Hank" Fontana. He's done time for fraud, assault, check kiting, possession of stolen goods and burglary.'

'Great – let's find out where our bad boy might be. Why don't you call Brooks and ask him to check on Collins' alibi at St. Regis. I'll run Fontana on the in-car unit.'

Kahn sat behind the wheel and began the computer database search on Fontana.

Outside Wagner paced up and down on Collins' drive, smoking another cigarette as he spoke with Brooks at the Precinct.

Kahn copied Fontana's address onto a sheet of paper, and handed it to Wagner when he climbed back into the car.

'Before we go visit Big Hank,' Wagner said, 'you and I have another stop we have to make first.'

'Yeah?' Kahn said. 'Where?'

'How quickly they forget,' Wagner said. He rolled down the window and flicked the cigarette butt into Collins' fountain. It lodged between the centaur's shoulder blades. 'To the Sagebrush Cantina. It's taco time.'

9

'So anyway,' Coombs said, 'when he got to the parking garage, he decided to stop and fight...'

The car radio crackled into life. 'Hey, boys and girls, Brooks here.'

'Wotcha got, Sarge?' said Albanese.

'Update on the mad mama and her daughter from the *Scarlet Mays* episode. They're in Ossing, New York, and they apparently haven't been anywhere in the last seventy-two hours. Keep hunting.'

'Roger that,' Albanese said. He took the turning onto Laurel Canyon, then looked at Coombs. 'So you were saying?'

'He obviously thought that I wouldn't cause too many problems. He turned on me, with an eight-inch pig-sticker in his right hand. I figured if I shot him in the head, the dumbass wouldn't feel it so I aimed for his fruit stand and told him I was going to blow his balls off in three seconds. Then I started counting. Apparently just the thought of losing his family jewels convinced him to give it up. Men. Go figure, huh?'

'Hey,' Albanese said. 'Um, guy here.'

'Make a note of it,' Coombs said.

Albanese took a hairpin past an Art Deco mansion behind iron gates, number 4240. From the numbered keypad, it looked to be broken up into apartments.

'Kowalski's should be on the right,' she said.

And there it was, with a unit car parked in the driveway opposite. Albanese pulled up out front, right up to the yellow tape which still stretched across the entrance. A stocky, short-haired young officer, who was sheltering under a pergola, approached the car and introduced herself as Tripucka.

'You missed the last of the press,' she said.

'I figured some of them would be sitting in the trees like vultures,' Albanese said.

'Tell me about it,' Tripucka said. 'Every call I got on the radio, someone would ask me what was said, what that code meant and so on.'

'You alone?' Coombs asked.

'No. There were a lot of guys here until about an hour ago. Now it's just me and Pete – I mean, Officer Donawald. He went to get us some lunch.'

Albanese checked his watch. 'It's a little

early, isn't it?'

'Not for Peter.'

Coombs soaked in as much of the air-conditioning as she could, then climbed out of the car.

'Herdez and Diaz were here earlier,' said Tripucka. 'They took a few statements from passers-by. Nothing much, but the guy who lives up in four-two-five-two heard a couple arguing around twelve-fifteen. Says it woke him up.'

'Thanks,' said Coombs. 'You get back in the shade.'

'Let's walk up the street a couple of houses,' said Albanese, 'then work our way down through the knock-knocks.' He sounded pissed.

'Knock-knocks?' said Coombs. 'Like the joke?'

'Yeah, a joke assignment. Knock-knock, who's there? Did you see anyone? No. Did you hear anyone? No. Is somebody on the squad pissed at you?'

Coombs hesitated. Was he referring to Sal? He had to be referring to Sal. Who else could it be? She feigned a look of surprise. 'Why do you say that?'

'I'm trying to find out why we got given this bullshit.'

Phew. 'Maybe it's because you got the new girl as your partner,' Coombs suggested. 'Don't newbies usually get the short end of the stick?'

'But I'm not a new guy...' Albanese stopped short and gave her an apologetic look. 'Hey, nothing personal. I was venting.'

The first few houses were just like Albanese said. In one the housekeeper answered, and she didn't speak English. In two others no one was home. As they walked down a steep section of asphalt to an expansive bungalow a few meters up the hill from Kowalski's, Coombs could feel her armpits sweating. Albanese wiped his forehead with a green silk handkerchief.

'What we need is a nice old lady to invite us in for homemade lemonade.'

Coombs rang the bell. A dog began yapping.

A female voice joined in with the barking. 'Quiet, Reginald. Quiet now. Hush. Who is it?'

'Maybe we'll get that lemonade after all,' said Coombs.

'Just open the door, Wanda,' a man's voice said.

'Who is it?'

'Police, ma'am,' said Coombs, over the dog's incessant yapping. She held up her badge and ID to the small window in the door. 'We'd like to ask you a few questions.'

From inside the voices and barking continued. 'It's the police, Vern.'

'Well, open the door, then.'

'How do we know it really is the police? Maybe it's somebody who wants to rape me.'

'It's a woman. A police woman. Didn't you see her badge? Open the door. No one wants to rape you. Even if it was Genghis Khan himself knocking on the door, you wouldn't be in danger of being raped.'

Coombs heard the sound of a lock being undone. Slowly, the door opened a few inches with the chain latch still in place. 'What is it?' the old woman asked. Her boney hand clutched a Chihuahua. The dog squirmed and growled and bared its small white incisors as the old woman leaned forward.

'Give me the damn dog,' the male voice inside said, but the old lady ignored his demand.

'Good afternoon,' Coombs said. 'Are you the homeowner?'

'Since May second, nineteen sixty-five,' she said.

'Nineteen sixty-six,' the man said. 'It was nineteen sixty-six.'

'You can't remember our anniversary. Don't pretend to know when we bought this house.'

'It's because the house still has value for me.'

'Could we get your names, please?' Coombs asked. She wasn't in the mood for marital squabbles.

'Wanda and Vernon Krueger,' the old woman said. 'Why do you need to know our names? Are we in trouble? If Vern did something, he isn't responsible for his actions.'

'Remember where you heard that, officers,' Vern said from somewhere behind her. 'Someday I may need witnesses.'

'Shut up. I was talking about your bladder.'

'No one is in trouble, Mrs. Krueger. I don't know if you are aware of it, but your neighbour Mr. Kowalski, the one that lives right behind you, was killed last night.'

'Oh my,' the lady said. 'I should have called the police when I heard those shots.'

'You heard shots? Coombs asked. She looked at Albanese. He shook his head.

'She heard nothing,' the lady's husband said. 'She's hard of hearing and crazier than a loon.'

'Shut up, Vern. Pay no attention to the old grouch. He needs his medication and he probably has his underwear on backwards. I did too hear something. I think it was around eleven o'clock. There were at least two shots. Maybe three. Then there was shouting and the sound of a car pulling away real fast.'

'You haven't seen eleven o'clock in thirty years, woman. Why do you want to lie to these policemen? You're telling them what you saw on *Matlock* at eight o clock.'

'You don't know. You were in your recliner, as usual. It's a miracle I heard anything with your snoring.'

'Thank you,' Albanese said. 'We'll look into it. If we need more information, we'll be back.'

'Is that all?' the old woman asked. 'Maybe I can tell you something else that is important. If I think a while, I bet I can remember what the killer looked like.'

'Let them go, for the love of...'

'You shut up, Vern.'

They left the couple bickering and approached the house directly in front of Kowalski's.

'Last one,' Albanese said. 'Let's go.'

As they approached the front door, a scent of baking bread filled the air. Wisteria vines with long lavender flowers covered the entrance archway. Coombs rang the bell and waited. A young woman with long straight brown hair and dressed like she had just left a sixties commune, slowly opened the door. Her finger was placed to her lips. 'Shh,' she said. 'The baby is sleeping.'

Coombs introduced herself and Albanese and explained why they were there. 'And your name is?' she asked.

'Rowena. Rowena Patchen. I heard sirens and saw the police lights this morning when I was feeding Melody. I didn't realize Mr. Kowalski had been killed. Of course, I don't poke my nose into other people's business but one hears things. The rumour around the neighborhood was that he was a pornographer. Is that true?'

'We're still investigating,' Albanese said.

'Whatever he did, no one deserves to be murdered. Can I ask – how was he killed?'

'We're still waiting for the medical examiner to give us details,' Coombs said. 'Did you happen to hear anything unusual or see anybody suspicious hanging around the last few days?'

'Unusual. I didn't know about unusual.'

'Maybe you saw a person you haven't seen before. That kind of thing,' Coombs said.

'It was nothing special, but last night my husband and I went out to dinner. When we came home around nine, there was a gray pickup truck parked over there near the black walnut tree. I didn't recognize it, but of course it could have been a visitor.'

'Did you happen to get the make of the truck?' Coombs asked.

'No. My husband might know. All I know is that it was gray and a pickup.'

'That helps. Was there anything else you might have seen? Did you see the driver of the truck, for instance?'

'No. I didn't see anyone.'

It wasn't much to go on, and Coombs could see a flicker of impatience at the corner of Albanese's mouth.

'Is there anything else?' she asked.

'Well, I don't know if this is important, but

there was a car over there at least two times in the last week or so. I told my husband about it. He said it was none of our business. We try to keep out of other people's business, you know?'

'Do you think we could come in for a minute, Mrs. Patchen, and get a statement from you?' Coombs asked.

'Well, alright,' she said. 'Just be quiet, please. I don't want to wake the baby.'

The inside of the house was immaculate and filled with the smell of baking bread. Two pies sat cooling on the counter. Nothing was out of place and everything sparkled. She led them to the kitchen. 'Is this okay?' she asked, gesturing to two stools next to the counter. She scooted several pots of fresh herbs to one side. Other herbs were drying in the window. 'Would you like some tea? I could put the kettle on. I'd offer you some pie but I think they are too warm to cut.'

'This will be fine,' Coombs said as she took a seat at the kitchen island. 'Everything smells wonderful but we've already eaten.' She took out her pad and pen. 'Can you describe the vehicle you saw across the street?'

'I don't know what kind it was, other than it was a sports car.'

'You don't know the make or model?'

'Like I said, I don't really know makes of cars or trucks. It did kind of look like the car my brother has. I could call him and find

out what kind he has. It has a pointy nose.'
She gestured with her hands, indicating that
the front of the car came to a point.

'Ah. A pointy nose? Like this?' Coombs
asked, and sketched an aerial view of the
front of a Corvette.

'Yes. That's it.'

'So the car you saw was a Corvette?'

'Yes. That's what my brother has, a
Corvette.'

'Very good. Did you see the license plate?'

'No.'

'Color?'

'That's easy. Bright red. A convertible.'

'A red convertible. Is there anything else?'

'Well, the car was red, but it also had a
yellow silhouette of a reclining naked woman
painted down one whole side of the body.'

'You didn't think that was worth mention-
ing?' said Albanese, with a hint of frustration.

Coombs shot him a look. 'A yellow silhouette?' she repeated.

'Yes.'

'It went the length of the car?'

'Yes.' She smiled. 'From the pointy front
to the back.'

Coombs shared a look with Albanese, who
rolled his eyes, and wondered just what
herbs Rowena Patchen was drying in the
window. But it didn't matter. They finally
had a lead and it didn't come from *Matlock*.

'You hungry?' asked Albanese, as they left

the house. 'It's just after twelve.'

'Not really,' Coombs said. 'My stomach's a little queasy. But go ahead if you are. I could sure use something cold to drink.'

'Diaz said there's a place right up the street that makes great sandwiches.'

'Fine with me.'

A few minutes later Coombs sat opposite Albanese in a booth at Dago Joe's. The place had been a Buffalo Bill's Bison Burger Barn at one time. That was obvious from its shape and blue roof. The chain had folded, and this one was now an independent Italian joint with some Spanish additions for the locals and, for some strange reason, Creole dishes like red beans and rice. It was a jumbled menu to be sure, but Albanese immediately chose a meatball sandwich. 'Always go Italian when you can,' he said.

Coombs sipped a Diet Pepsi and watched him eat. Marinara sauce and gooey cheese dripped freely from between the Italian bread, yet Albanese somehow managed to remain immaculate. He was either gay or one of the neatest straight guys she'd ever met. Considering that he had already made a couple of suggestive comments, she would bet on the latter.

'So, tell me a little about yourself,' he said. 'I hear you used to work here.'

'If you mean the LAPD, then yes. There's not much to tell, though. I worked in Juvenile

Crime in Beverly Hills for a short while. There was a bunch of robberies, burglaries and muggings going on in the neighborhood so they assigned me to work with ... a guy from Robbery. A few months later I got a chance to go to the FBI at Quantico so I did. Now I'm back.'

'That's it?'

'Isn't that enough?'

Albanese dabbed his lips with a paper napkin. She couldn't help but notice that he held her eye a little too long. 'For now, I guess.' He stuffed the last bit of onion into his mouth and wiped the crumbs from his hands. 'You about ready?'

'I'm waiting on you.' She smiled. He wanted a little more information. That was easy to see. He wanted to know where she lived, and if she was married or seeing anyone. But it was too early for getting that tight with anyone. Almost anyone.

10

Reyes and Wallace drove quietly along Hollywood Boulevard until Wallace finally broke the silence. 'It's kind of funny how two people can look at something and see two totally different things, isn't it?'

'Something particular you're thinking about?'

'Sadie Monaghan. Kowalski was porking her at fifteen and got her into porn before she was eighteen, yet she was grateful. Did you hear her talking about him? She made him sound like a freakin' hero. Yet I look at that same scenario and see child abuse.'

'Yeah, well, how long a minute is depends on which side of the bathroom door you're on.'

Wallace shook her head and looked at him. 'I think you're hanging around with Brooks too much. That sounds like something he'd say.'

'I'm just saying, sometimes you do what you have to do to survive.'

They drove on in silence for a few more minutes, as Reyes worked out how he could broach the next subject.

'Hey, Phil, I know we're under the gun on this case, but I did come in on my day off. Could you give me ten minutes to find something for my kid's birthday present? Balboa's Toys is right up here on Caheunga. They should have something good – something Nando would like.'

Wallace sighed. 'Sure.'

'I appreciate it,' said Reyes, taking a right turn onto North Caheunga Boulevard toward the store. 'It's right up there,' he said as the radio hissed.

'Assault in progress. The manager of the Mekong Massage Parlor reports a client being assaulted. Any officer in the area of Rampart and Third respond. See Rosie.'

'That's too far for us to get there in time,' Reyes said. 'Even if we wanted to.'

'Yeah. Let one of the patrols pick it up,' Wallace said.

Reyes parked the car in a no parking zone and flipped the blinkers to the on position. 'You coming in?' he asked. 'I could use some help with this.'

'Sorry, I haven't got a clue. I'd probably get a gift card.'

'His mom would have a shit-fit. She'd say it was a thoughtless gift.' Reyes opened the door and half-stepped out. 'Come on,' he said. 'Give me a hand.'

'Oh, alright,' Wallace said. 'Let's just do it quickly.'

Reyes searched the toys in the window as he walked by. He caught a reflection of Wallace's face. It was obvious she didn't want to be doing this. He'd have to make it quick.

An electronic bell rang as they entered the store. 'Can I help you?' a teenager asked. His nametag read: 'Balboa's Toys – Brad at your service'.

'I'm looking for a birthday present for a seven-year-old,' Reyes said.

'Boy or girl, or doesn't it matter?'

'It matters. Of course it matters. Jesus. It's

for my son.'

Brad didn't flinch. He asked several questions about Fernando's interests and suggested a number of presents. None of them struck Reyes as the right one.

'We've got to get going, Sal,' Wallace said. 'How about a bike?'

'A bike?' Reyes said. 'Yeah. That's it. A bike. Do you have bikes, Brad?'

Though the selection was limited, Reyes found the perfect bicycle. It was purple with pictures of Barney on it. 'He loves that show,' Reyes said. 'He used to watch it all the time, you know, before...'

'Yeah, I know,' Wallace said. 'Do you have one of those still in a box?' she asked.

Brad brought one from the storeroom. Reyes put the purchase on his charge card, grabbed the box and hurried to the car. He slipped it in the trunk and hopped behind the wheel. 'Thanks,' he said. 'That's a great gift. Nando and I can go bike-riding together. It's perfect.'

'Glad I could help,' Wallace said. Her phone rang and she flipped it open. 'Hey, Ray, what's going on?'

Reyes listened to her side of the conversation.

'Uh-huh, sure did, but we were too far away ... no shit ... we'll get on it. Tell them to hold on until we get there.' She hung up.

'What's up?' said Reyes.

'We need to get over to the Mekong Massage Parlor,' said Wallace. 'The unit who responded has just called for an ambulance – for none other than Trey Brightman.'

Reyes hit the sirens and headed for the Mekong, as Wallace typed in a request for information on Trey Brightman on the in-car computer. They arrived to see the ambulance parked in the street outside behind two squad cars. A crowd had gathered. Two officers were trying to keep the access to the massage parlor open. One was talking to the ambulance crew.

'Here ya go,' Wallace said, pointing at the computer screen. Reyes looked at the grinning face of a handsome, square-jawed man. 'Not much on him. Minor shit. Marijuana possession. A couple of traffic tickets.'

Reyes pulled aside his jacket to show his badge clip as they headed into the parlor. He led the way through hanging beads into a small office area. It was decorated in red and gold with stylized Asian dragons and hanging lanterns casting a glow on the furnishings and bamboo-colored walls. Officer Si Townsend was talking on his radio and gestured with his head as they approached.

'In the back,' he said. 'Second door on the left.'

As soon as Reyes pushed open the door, a small, middle-aged Asian woman was in his face.

'You arrest crazy woman!' she screeched.

'And you are?' Wallace asked.

'Tran Ngoc Minh. This my place. That woman crazy mad. You arrest her now. She ruin my business. I sue.'

'Calm down,' Wallace said. 'What woman are you talking about?'

'That woman who attack my customers.'

Townsend appeared at the door. 'The suspect, a Vera Yelland, is being held in room three to prevent further problems with the owner,' he said. 'We got a call saying to hold off on everything until you arrived.'

Wallace nodded. 'Well, let us see what's what, Tran ... no...'

'You call me Rosie.'

'Okay, Rosie,' Wallace said. 'Townsend, can you tell us what happened?'

'Sure. According to Rosie, a woman we have since identified as Yelland burst in here and assaulted one of the clients, a Trey Brightman with her high-heel shoe. Whacked him in the head.'

'And where is Brightman now?'

'Forston has them both in room three – down the hall. That's where the alleged assault took place.'

'Let's go, Sal,' Wallace said.

'You arrest her. She crazy mad person,' Rosie said. 'She number ten I tell you.'

'Number ten?' Reyes asked.

'You bet. Number ten. No good.'

105

Wallace went first into massage room three. A man Reyes immediately recognized from the computer picture as Trey Brightman sat on the table, a towel around his waist and a bloody hand towel pushed against his scalp. A young Asian girl was attempting to bandage the wound but Brightman was uncooperative and resisting her efforts, grimacing every time she touched him. He looked up as Wallace and Reyes entered the room.

Standing to the side was Jim Forston holding on to a very angry redhead in cuffs. Her breasts pushed against the tight fabric of a revealing silk blouse as she strained against his grip.

Wallace stood over Brightman. 'I'm Detective Wallace and this is Detective Reyes. You're Trey Brightman?'

'Yeah.'

Wallace turned to the redhead. 'And you are?'

'Vera Yelland, and I'm going to sue this Nazi for police brutality.'

'Uh-huh,' Wallace said. 'And what's your name, miss?' she said, tapping the Asian woman on the shoulder.

'I Maisie.'

'Alright. Let's start with you, Mr. Brightman. Do you want to tell me what happened?'

Brightman shot an angry stare at Yelland. 'Nothing, okay. I already told that guy,' he

106

said, gesturing toward Forston. 'Maisie, get me a cigarette, chop-chop.'

The girl said nothing. She put the bandages on the massage table and stepped over to a small square table stocked with boxes and bottles. She lit a cigarette and brought it back for Brightman. He put it in his mouth, took a drag and blew the smoke toward Yelland. Reyes stepped forward, plucked it from his hand and extinguished the butt beneath his foot.

'Don't make your day even worse with an arrest, Mr. Brightman.'

Wallace spoke to Yelland. 'How about you, Vera?' she said. 'Do you have anything you'd like to say?'

'Yes,' she said. 'Could you remove these handcuffs, please? They hurt.'

Wallace ignored the request. 'Jim, could you take Miss Maisie down the hall and see what she remembers?'

Forston stepped over and took Maisie by the arm. A look of fear came over her face. She looked at Brightman but he just stared back. 'Come on,' Forston said, and escorted her out of the room.

'So neither one of you wants to tell me what happened?' Wallace said. 'The lady who owns this joint wants you arrested, Miss Yelland. I don't know what you've got going with Mr. Brightman, but with Rosie willing to press charges, I don't need his complaint to hold and charge you.'

'I didn't do anything. Ask him,' she said, pointing with her head at Brightman.

'Look,' Brightman said. 'I was face down. Maisie was busy giving me a massage, so she didn't see anything. I felt this sharp pain and when I sat up, no one was here except Maisie and my old friend, Vera. Obviously it was someone else who attacked me.'

'So the three of you were in the room but no one saw your attacker?'

'I don't know. Yeah, I guess that's about it,' Brightman said. 'The bottom line is, none of us did it and none of us saw anything.'

'Do you always go for a massage the day after your business partner's found dead?' asked Reyes.

'It's never happened before,' said Brightman. 'Zane and I were partners, not friends, as I have already told one of your lackeys this morning.'

Reyes stepped in the hall and signaled the EMTs to come in. Then he walked back to the lobby where Jim Forston was jotting info into his notebook. 'Get anything out of little Maisie?'

'Not a peep,' Forston said. 'She keeps saying, "Me not see" and then something in Vietnamese. I finally asked Rosie to come over and help me translate.'

Reyes turned to Rosie. 'Well?'

Rosie looked at Maisie. 'She say she make

a mistake. Maybe she wrong.'

'I see,' Reyes said. 'Okay, boys, it looks like everybody's happy. You know that you're going to get a write-up for running a disorderly establishment, don't you, Rosie? A public nuisance?'

'I fix,' Rosie said. 'We be good you betcha. Special deal for police. You come back. You see.'

Wallace and Reyes returned to their squad car. Reyes signaled that they were back. 'Car zero-one-one. Ten-eighteen.' He released the send button. 'Okay, what was all that about?'

'I don't know.'

'Good. I thought I missed something.'

'I think we did miss something.'

'What?'

'I don't know. Rosie wanted to hang Yelland. Ten minutes later she says it was all a mistake.'

'Do you think it has anything to do with Kowalski?'

'I don't know. Maybe. Maybe Brightman is a big tipper. But a guy's gotta be pretty cocky to talk waltz around the streets of Hollywood the night after murdering his partner.' He dropped the car into gear, eased away from the curb. 'You know what I think?'

'Go on.' said Wallace.

'I think he's just an asshole, and I don't want to be investigating an asshole's love life. My own is bad enough.'

11

Wagner pulled into the parking lot outside the Sunset Lodge on North Berendo and slowly drove through as Kahn verified the address on the in-car computer. 'Yup, this is it. I'll tell Brooks we're here.'

Kahn called headquarters. 'Okay, Ray, we're in the parking lot at Henry Fontana's apartment. Have we got a go to enter?'

'No, wait for backup. This guy could be our killer. A third strike and he's out. If he's there, bring him in clean. Don't take the door off. And be careful. Three-timers always resist.'

'Okay,' Kahn said. He hung up, then peered up at the apartment building. 'Pretty straightforward,' he said. 'Front door, back stairs.'

Wagner nodded, did a U-turn and headed back to the front of the building. 'Does Brooks ever take a day off?' he asked. 'I swear to God I don't remember him ever taking a stinking day off. Not one. It's unnatural.'

'He's like a priest. You know, always on duty.'

'It's inhuman.'

'He's just devoted. I don't see Fontana's truck. Do you?'

Wagner looked around. 'Nope, but that doesn't mean he isn't home.'

'I know. I was only saying I didn't see it.'

Wagner drummed the steering wheel. A few minutes passed, then he looked in the rearview mirror. 'Backups's here,' he said.

A black-and-white cruiser braked alongside them.

'Here we go,' said Kahn.

It was Tina Lantz and Tibor Martin. They looked like some sort of comedy act; she was struggling to reach 5ft and Tibor was pushing 6ft 4in. Kahn showed them the picture of Fontana. 'This is the guy we're looking for. He lives in apartment ten.' He pointed to a green second-floor door at the corner. 'This joker is wanted in a homicide investigation so be careful. He's already had two strikes so it's likely that he'll be desperate and won't come easy. We don't want anybody getting hurt. Pick a good spot by the back stairs. If this son-of-a-bitch comes out of a door, a window or a pipe, take him.'

'Sure thing,' said Martin, and strode off down the path to the rear of the building, Tina trotting beside him.

'Okay, let's hit it,' Wagner said, already drawing his gun.

Kahn followed him up the steps and into the shaded balcony corridor. They walked quickly along past the front window and took positions either side of the door.

'I don't hear anybody,' Wagner said.

Kahn drew his Beretta. 'Ready?' he said.

Wagner nodded and gave him a thumbs-up.

Kahn pounded on the door. 'Henry Fontana. Open up. This is the police.' Silence. He looked at Wagner and shrugged, then knocked again. 'Fontana. LAPD. Open the door now.'

Wagner peered through the window. 'No movement. No lights. No sounds.'

The door to apartment eleven opened a few inches. Kahn spun and pointed his weapon; Wagner did likewise. A pudgy, pink-faced man in a Dodgers cap appeared, stared wide-eyed and backed up into his apartment. 'Easy,' he said. 'Easy.'

'Stay inside, sir,' Kahn said. He backed up and lowered his gun. Wagner radioed the officers guarding the rear. 'Anything back there?' he asked.

'Negative,' Lantz replied.

'Easy,' the man said again from inside number eleven and slowly opened the door a little further. 'Don't point those things at me.'

'Stay inside, sir,' Kahn said.

'But aren't you looking for Mr. Fontana?'

Kahn glanced at Wagner who nodded.

'Okay, step out slowly, sir,' Kahn said.

The man poked his head out, then pulled off his cap, wiping his brow with his forearm. 'I was just going to tell you that if you're

112

looking for Mr. Fontana, he's not there. I haven't heard anything for a while now.' A woman's voice from inside the man's apartment said, 'Since right after breakfast.'

'You heard him at breakfast this morning?' Kahn asked.

'Yes. He hadn't been home for well over a week. Maybe ten days. It was very nice. Peace and quiet. We were hoping that maybe he had moved away. Then this morning, he came home. Banging around as usual. It put my mother on edge, I'll tell you. She couldn't enjoy her oatmeal. Anyway, we heard the door slam and suddenly it was quiet again.'

Kahn holstered his weapon but signaled Wagner to keep his at the ready. 'Do you know Mr. Fontana, sir?'

'I see him once in a while. I know he's not in now because when he is, he has his stereo set on full blast and all bass. It shakes our walls like Joshua at Jericho. I asked him once to be a little more considerate. I told him my mother lives with me. He told me to go fuck a chicken.'

Wagner laughed then feigned a cough. 'Sorry. Did you call the police? Noise pollution is against the law.'

'Oh, yes, that's good advice. I call the police. They tell Fontana that his neighbors think he is being too loud. The cops leave and then he comes after me and my mother. I think not.'

'Tell you what, Mr...?'

'You're not going to tell him we talked, are you?'

'No. I promise,' Kahn said.

'Heflin. Randy Heflin.'

'Mr. Heflin, here's my card. If you could give me a call when your neighbor comes home, I'd sure appreciate it. And I promise he won't know who called.'

Mr. Heflin took the card nervously and inspected it. 'Okay, if you promise. I don't want to get involved with that crude individual.' He put his cap back on, went inside and closed the door.

'Did you hear a call for help?' Wagner asked, pointing at Fontana's door with his gun. 'I think it's coming from inside this apartment.'

Kahn frowned. 'That's not going to work this time, Harlen. No one's home.'

'Maybe Fontana kidnapped somebody and they struggled to get their gag free and now they're calling for help.'

'Come on. One slip-up on this case and we'll be writing parking tickets for the rest of our careers. Seriously.'

'I still think I hear something,' Wagner said. 'Maybe he's torturing cats.' He jiggled the handle as he rammed his shoulder firmly against the door. 'It'd go down easy. Hmm? Hmm?'

The door to apartment eleven swung open

again. Wagner pointed his gun, with a guilty look on his face.

'Easy, boys, it's me again, Randy Heflin.'

'Mr. Heflin,' Kahn said, exhaling. 'When you know there is police action going on outside your place, you really should be very careful about any sudden movements like opening your door. It's best to stay inside.'

'Oh. Sorry,' he said. 'Mother said I should mention that Mr. Fontana likes to hang out at the Mexican Smuggler over behind the Chinese Theater. You might try there.'

'The Mexican Smuggler? How does your mother know that's where Mr. Fontana likes to hang out, Mr. Heflin?'

The Mexican Smuggler wasn't exactly a dive but it was heading in that direction. It was a throwback place that allowed smoking and still offered an unannounced happy hour. He and Wagner had stopped in for a beer once or twice before without much concern. Of course, they were both armed.

'I'm a pearl diver there,' he said. 'And my mother is a cook.'

'Pearl diver?' Wagner asked. Kahn shrugged.

'A dishwasher. I work in their kitchen. I don't think Mr. Fontana knows we work there. And I don't want him to.'

'You have my word,' Kahn said.

Heflin closed the door to his apartment. Kahn could hear the dead bolt being turned and the latch fastened.

'Want to release the patrol and head over there?' Wagner asked.

'No. Let's call it in first and see what Brooks has to say. I can't believe he'll authorize just the two of us to cover it.'

'Don, if we're going to keep the patrol, we may as well have a marching band lead us in. The rats inside will be gone before we open the doors to spring the trap. Let the troops go. After we assess the situation, we can always call for assistance if we think we need it.'

'Why not clear it now?'

Wagner rolled his eyes. 'You're becoming a real wuss. Okay. I'll tell you what. We'll call it in, but let me talk to Brooks.'

'If you want,' Kahn said. 'I'll get the guys from around the back.'

They descended the steps. Wagner headed for the car. Kahn walked toward the back. Tibor Martin and Tina Lantz were leaning up against the step rail, eyes to the floor above. 'Hey, guys,' he said. 'Our boy apparently isn't in. Why don't you pull around the front? We're calling in to see what our next step is going to be.'

Tina looked relieved, Tibor a little disappointed.

When Kahn reached the car again, Wagner was climbing out.

'Okay, worrywart, we're good to go.'

'Really? Brooks okayed the two of us?'

'More or less.'

Lantz and Martin stopped the squad car next to Wagner. Martin rolled down the driver's window. 'So, what's up?'

'You can resume your normal patrol,' said Kahn. 'We're going to check out another site. If we think we need help, we'll call.'

'See you later then,' Martin said. He rolled up the window and pulled away.

'I'll drive,' said Kahn, climbing into the driver's side. He waited until Wagner got in. 'You're sure this is how we're supposed to do this? No backup?'

'Everything is covered. You think I'd bull-shit you?' Wagner lit a cigarette and exhaled. 'We're only going to check things out. Trust me, everything will be fine.' Kahn raised his eyebrows. 'Seriously, do you think I'd do anything that would put my partner in jeopardy?'

'Until this morning, I'd have said no. After you got a look at Coombs, I'm not so sure.'

'Hey, I couldn't do that if Miss Commando was my partner.'

'Do what?' asked Kahn, confused. Then the smell hit him. 'You son-of a-bitch,' he said as he lowered all the car's windows. 'You need to quit eating Spanish food if that's what it does to you.'

12

'A naked woman?' said Brooks over the car radio.

Coombs smothered a laugh. Albanese grinned and repeated himself. 'That's right. A red Corvette with the yellow silhouette of a naked woman on it. It might be registered as a two-tone.'

'It's that kind of day, huh?' Brooks said. 'Your computer goes out and then you ask me to run a red Corvette displaying porn. Anything else?'

'There's a second vehicle,' said Albanese, 'but the description is kind of vague. A gray truck. Maybe a Dodge.'

'Maybe?' said Brooks.

'The witnesses wouldn't swear to the year, make or anything else for that matter.'

Brooks sighed. 'I'll run the car.'

'Would you like to get some coffee or head back to the station?' Coombs said.

'I don't care either way.'

'Let's just go in, then. Maybe we can lend somebody else a hand. Doesn't Ray have a ton of videos to look through? Maybe we can help with that.'

'Um. Yeah, I guess.' Albanese drove toward

the station, keeping his eyes open for the red Corvette and a gray pickup of unknown year, make and model. 'So, do you have your own place?' he asked.

'I have a house over on Maplewood,' she replied. 'It used to belong to my parents but they're both dead now. That's one of the reasons I came back.'

You idiot, Albanese cursed himself. 'I see,' he said. 'Sorry for your loss. Was their passing sudden?'

'They were killed in a hit-and-run accident. Witnesses said the car was speeding and driving erratically. It T-boned my folks' car and drove on.'

'Oh, man, that's too bad. I mean, it really is. I'm sorry. Did they catch the guy?'

'Yeah. The "guy" was a sixteen-year-old girl who was drunk as a pirate. When they found the car a short distance away, she was passed out on the front seat and naked from the waist down. No one knows what happened exactly because she claimed she couldn't remember a thing. I do know that she escaped without a scratch. She also had no idea where the rest of her clothes were. The investigation suggested someone else might have been driving and she couldn't remember one way or another. It's still unresolved. I try not to talk about it too much, you know? It's still a little too fresh and painful.'

'Sure. I understand. I'm sorry. I didn't

mean to bring up bad memories.'

'It's alright.' she said. She turned her gaze out the window.

Albanese stared at the traffic. *Nice job, you dumb-ass,* he thought. *Of all the freakin' topics to break the ice, you pick that one. How are your dead parents? Would you like to go out tonight?* 'So, what exactly did you do with the FBI?' he said eventually. 'I mean, if you can tell me.'

'I was going through a program, which was flunking out a lot of potential law enforcement agents because they failed to qualify on their firearms. The Bureau instituted a sort of recycle program and the numbers of successful candidates went up dramatically. Someone decided to expand that concept to the whole training program. I was selected to be a participant. It covered everything but I found my niche in the high tech part of it. Like I said, though, I felt like I had to come home.'

'The FBI's loss is our gain,' said Albanese, flashing her his best smile.

She barely smiled back. 'Thanks.'

Albanese drove the rest of the way in silence, and pulled into the station's parking lot. 'Why do I get the feeling we're going to be at this investigation for a while? The more we press, the further away things seem to be. On any other day, while Brooks looked for those cars, I'd have gone and got a cup of coffee or something. Today, you feel guilty if you take a break.'

'We can only do so much. We had a slogan at the FBI that kind of applies.'

'What was that?'

'We can only do so much.' She smiled. 'I'm going to let Brooks know we're here. Maybe somebody can look at our computer.'

Albanese went into the locker room and washed his face. *Drop a little hint here,* he thought, *a little innuendo there. Who knows what she might respond to? Don't move too fast. Stay away from the dead parent thing.* He considered changing his shirt but decided it wasn't worth the effort. A half-hour outside and he'd be soaked again. He splashed on a little cologne, straightened his tie and headed back to his desk. Half way there Coombs met him heading in the opposite direction.

'A patrol spotted our red Corvette about five minutes after we called in,' she said. 'That's like two minutes ago. It was in the parking lot of the Red Giraffe. They were going to wait for us but got a call and had to leave. They let Brooks know right away.'

'We need to get a better clientele of criminals,' Albanese said. 'Somebody that hangs out at Les Deux instead of the Red Giraffe.'

'I haven't been to either, but I'vc heard how fancy Les Deux is. I'm assuming then that the Red Giraffe is a dive?'

'Strip club. So, who's our boy?'

'The car is registered to Jermaine Orwell.'

Coombs checked the sheet Brooks had handed her 'It appears that the circle continues. He's a casting agent mostly. Some modeling gigs.'

'Let me see,' Albanese said. 'His car was seen at Kowalski's house and at a strip club, so I'm going to take a wild guess that his primary business is working with porn stars. Am I right?'

'I don't know. He owns a casting company called, and you're going to love this, Yellow Lady. He doesn't have a record. Brooks said a couple of the guys who work vice told him Orwell tends toward the shady end of the business but hasn't done anything illegal unless you count being involved in the porn business.'

'Maybe he hasn't been caught yet.'

They exited the building and headed for their car. 'Dammit. I've lived in L.A. virtually my whole life and I don't remember a day this hot,' Albanese said. 'It feels like someone put a glass dome over the city.' He eased into the driver's seat, cursed the boiling steering wheel. He reached into the side compartment on the door and pulled out his driving gloves.

Coombs stared.

'What? They're practical and they make me look cool. Where are we headed?'

Coombs laughed. 'Our man has an office near Los Feliz. Shall we go check out that

122

hot car of his?'

Traffic was light. They sailed toward Orwell's office, not far from the Sandy Vista Business Mall. Albanese pulled the cruiser into the parking lot slowly, savoring the air con.

The area looked to be mostly professional offices. Physical therapists, insurance agents, tax consultants, investment brokers. But there it was, the second-to-last office, a talent agency. The windows were tinted to keep out the sun, but over the years, the trees along the edge of the parking lot had grown and now cast their shadows over the front of the building.

'I don't see the car,' Coombs said, 'but check out the door.' A yellow silhouette of a reclining woman was painted on the glass along with the address and the name of the business. Yellow Lady Agency.

'You never know,' Albanese said. 'Maybe he has a garage behind the building or something. Let's go inside and see what's happening in the exciting world of the casting couch.'

An electronic bell sounded as they entered the small but attractive office. Equally attractive were two early-twenties females seated near the door. The blonde was dressed in hot pants; the brunette in a mini-mini-skirt. Both wore halter tops. They smiled at Albanese and checked out Coombs with a critical eye.

The office was decorated in shades of orange, and spice candles burned, adding a pleasant fragrance to the room. The walls were covered in photographs of male and female actors, the males to the left and the women to the right.

A matronly woman with graying black hair was sitting behind a sliding-glass window. She smiled as they approached. 'Good afternoon. May I help you?'

Coombs held up her police ID. 'I'm Detective Coombs. This is Detective Albanese. We'd like to see Mr. Jermaine Orwell. Are we in the right place?'

'Yes. Yes, this is his office but he's with clients right now. Not here,' she added. 'He's out of the building.' She was obviously nervous, fumbling to explain the absence of her boss.

'Uh-huh. Do you happen to know when he's expected back?' Albanese asked.

The woman's slightly pudgy cheeks had taken on a pink flush. Was it because they were cops or was something else going on?

'It's hard to say,' she said, 'but he thought he would be back right about now. But he isn't.'

'In that case, we'll wait,' he said. He popped open his tin of Myntz. 'Want one?' he said, offering a mint candy to the receptionist.

'No. Thank you,' she said. 'Do you want

124

me to try and reach him on his cell phone? If it's an emergency, I'm sure he wouldn't mind if I interrupted him.'

'No, don't do that,' Albanese said. 'We'd kind of like to surprise him.'

13

'You cleared this with Brooks, did you?' Wallace asked.

'Phil, I'm hurt that you would even suggest I didn't follow procedure,' Wagner said.

'Gee, that sounded sincere,' Reyes said.

'This one is ours, Sally. We needed you or I could have called for the meter maids. Easy in, easy out.'

'You needed me?' Reyes asked. 'This is gonna be good.'

'If you got the okay,' Wallace said, 'then let's quit yapping and do this. What's the plan?'

Kahn looked at his partner and gestured to him, suggesting it was his idea, his call.

'We got a tip that Fontana could be inside the Mexican Smuggler. When we got here, we found his truck, that gray Toyota over there,' Wagner said, pointing to a pickup parked in the street. 'What we're going to do is send somebody into the Mexican Smuggler to see if Fontana is really inside. It's a bit of a dive so we need somebody who doesn't appear to be out of place. That's why Albanese and Coombs were out. Too classy. We need someone who looks like they might be a person of questionable character.' Wagner stepped up to Reyes, face-to-face, his head cocked to one side. 'So, Sally old boy, how about it? Can you be seedy for us?'

'Usted tonta mierda.' Reyes shook his head.

'Wagner's just giving you a hard time, Sal,' Kahn said. 'But it really should be you who goes in. We've been in there before so the odds are someone would recognize us as cops. Phil walking in would be kind of strange, especially her going in alone. They may not figure her for a cop but she is not typical solo clientele. It really has to be you, Sal, no offense intended.'

Wagner grinned at Reyes over Kahn's shoulder. 'Well?' he said. 'You going into the Smuggler for us, Seedy Gonzalez?'

'I'll go. I don't have a problem with that,' Reyes said. 'But one of these days...' He turned his radio off, split it into two parts, slipping the clip section into his jacket pocket, the handheld into his pants pocket. He handed his jacket and holster to Wallace, then rolled up his sleeves. 'Well, how do I look?'

'Not much of a change,' Wagner said.

'I'm assuming you have a leg piece?'

Wallace said.

Reyes tapped his calf.

'Pull your shirt out. Unbutton it,' Wallace said.

'Okay, yeah, that's a little better,' Wagner said. He handed Reyes the photo from the file. 'Here's Fontana's pic. If he's in there, find a place you can call from without being heard and tell us his location. You know, at the bar, east-side booth, table in the middle of the floor, that kind of thing.'

'Yeah. I understand English,' Reyes said. 'Then what?'

'Okay There are three doors. The front one and a side door near the bar. The third door is through the storeroom in the back. Each of us will cover one of those. The two who get the side and front doors will come in. We announce and take his ass. If he bolts, the only door available is the back. Whoever is back there will take him down when he comes out.'

'Just us four?' Wallace said. 'Shouldn't we get a couple of uniforms?'

'Jesus Christ, Phil. The guy may not even be inside. Why the hell do we need an army down here to check out one bar?' Wagner said. 'Somebody will see the activity, alert the people inside, and the next thing you know, Fontana's on his way out of town.'

'All I'm saying is, what with the media focus on this case, it would be better to cover all our bases. Err on the side of caution.'

'We got the go-ahead on this one, Phil,' Wagner said. 'But you're the ranking officer on the scene. Take over if you want to.' He placed his hands on his hips.

Wallace glanced at Reyes.

He shrugged, then said, 'It's okay with me.'

'What more do you need?' Wagner asked.

'Alright,' she said. 'Fine.'

'I'll take the front door,' Wagner directed. 'Don, you cover the side door. Phil, you take the back.'

Reyes walked toward the Mexican Smuggler while Wagner, Kahn and Wallace moved the unmarked squad cars closer. Wallace parked alongside the Toyota on the street side, Kahn behind it.

Reyes stood behind a tree, out of sight so that anyone entering or exiting the Smuggler wouldn't see him. The others took their assigned places. He gave them a quick wave, walked across the parking lot and stepped inside.

Heads turned to see who had entered the sanctuary. The door closed behind him and sent the inside of the place back into an eerie darkness. Reyes' eyes adjusted to the lack of light. He had figured the place would be nearly empty but instead found a room full of gargoyles, hunched over drinks, their stony stares suggesting that they just wanted to be left alone. A week's pay said that half of the people in there knew what the inside of Pelican Bay looked like and the other half would find out one day. A few of them would be packing weapons of some kind – knives mostly. This could get butt-ugly if he wasn't careful.

A fog of tobacco smoke muted the bright colors from a half-dozen neon signs that promoted beer and cigarettes. The main room was filled with round tables and straight-backed chairs. The walls of dark wood paneling were lit by a dozen small sconces, each holding a flickering amber lightbulb. The walls were sparsely decorated.

A cigarette machine and a jukebox sat against the far wall, separating the doorways to the men and women's restrooms. As far as he could see, there weren't any female customers. Twenty feet to the left of the cigarette machine was the side exit. To the right of the jukebox and past the men's room, the main room made a ninety-degree turn and became a games room complete with a pool table and numerous pinball and video machines.

Reyes took a stool at the bar. 'Beer,' he said when the bartender moved closer. 'Whatever's on tap.' He spun slowly around and looked over the room.

The ones with warrants were probably checking him out. *Move slowly.* No point in getting everybody excited. Damn, this place was worse than Harlen said. It was a dirty, stinking dive. Of course, that dickwad probably felt right at home in here.

The bartender put the beer on the counter. 'Three-fifty,' he said, his hand resting on the bar, inches from the sweaty glass as though poised to yank it back if he didn't see the money. He was a large, strong-looking man, more bouncer than bartender. His head was shaved and he sported a neat, close-cut beard.

Reyes dropped a five on the counter. 'Here ya go,' he said. 'Got change for the jukebox?'

'Sure,' he said. A minute later he was back with six quarters.

'Thanks,' Reyes said. He stepped off the stool and moved toward the jukebox, glancing around the room as casually as he could. There were a couple of white guys that were too old to be Fontana. He didn't care about the three black guys. One by one he eliminated patrons until there remained four white guys with their backs to him, any of whom might be Fontana. He couldn't maneuver enough without being obvious. He took his time studying the jukebox, then selected a couple of Santana tracks.

Reyes returned to his seat at the bar. He took another look over his shoulder. Should he wait them out, or leave and explain the situation to the others? He took a sip of the beer. *Aw, fuck it.* He gestured for the bartender to come back. Quietly, he pulled out his badge and the mug shot of Fontana. 'Seen this guy lately? His name's Fontana – Henry Fontana.'

'Gee, you're a cop. Who'd have guessed?' He threw a bar towel over his shoulder. 'Ain't seen him.'

Reyes checked to see if the bartender's comments had alarmed anyone. The music would have covered his words for sure. 'Here's the thing. Fontana's truck is parked outside. Also in the parking lot is a SWAT team ready to come through the doors when I give them the nod. Things could get kind of nasty. Or you can take a look at the picture and give me a straight answer – quietly. Then we might be able to do this without anybody getting hurt.' The bartender stared at Reyes, weighing up his options. 'And your place won't get all busted up.'

The bartender slowly looked around the room before returning his focus to Reyes. 'Look – officer – most of the people in here have already made you, I'm sure.' He spoke in a low voice. 'You guarantee you ain't gonna fuck up my place?'

'I'll try not to,' he said. 'Have you seen him?'

'He's right behind you,' he said. 'The guy with the blue shirt and leather vest. He's got his back to you and he's sitting with some guy named Tinto or Tonto or something like that.'

'Tinto? Is that his first name or last name or what?'

'I don't know. Maybe it was Tonto. He's a friend of Henry's. I think that's what he called him.'

Reyes casually turned on his stool. Fontana was sitting hunched over a table with a skinny, unshaven male probably in his late twenties. Neither man looked at Reyes. *So far, so good.*

Reyes walked to the men's room, checked that the stalls were empty and pulled out his handheld radio. 'Fontana's sitting at a table with at least one other guy. Some guy named Tonto.'

'Can we take them?' Wagner said. 'Any obstacles?'

'I think it's an easy takedown, but be advised that the place is pretty packed. When you come through the front door, Fontana will be slightly to your right. I can cover from across the room. Kahn, when you come through the side door, look toward your right. Give me to the count of ten to take up a good spot, then come on in.'

Wagner and Kahn acknowledged. Reyes pulled the door to the men's room open and stepped back into the bar area. Fontana's table was empty. *What the...* Reyes glanced across the room. His panic subsided for the moment when he saw Fontana and Tonto leaning on the bar talking with the bartender.

132

Then all three men shifted their gaze to Reyes. Tonto walked away, heading for the side door. Fontana started to follow his partner but kept his eyes locked on Reyes.

Reyes quickly glanced to check the movement he sensed to his left. The bartender was gone. Several patrons were rising from their chairs. He looked back toward Fontana in time to see his hand moving toward his waist.

'Police,' Reyes said. 'Everyone down.'

There was a surge of people toward both of the doors. Furniture scraped on the floor. Chairs were knocked over. A few patrons fell to the floor for cover. Most ran toward the exits.

'Everybody get down!' Reyes yelled. 'Get down!'

Tonto tipped a table over and ducked behind it. Fontana reached the end of the bar, ten feet or so from the side door, spun and aimed a Glock at Reyes.

14

Jermaine Orwell removed a tortoiseshell cigarette-holder from his mouth and exhaled as he greeted his receptionist. 'Hello, Mrs. LaBette. Any good news today?'

133

The receptionist held up several pink slips of paper. 'These are your phone messages,' she said. 'The two young ladies seated over them are actors looking for representation.' LaBette looked at Albanese and Coombs. 'And these two...'

Orwell snatched the messages, turned and held up a hand indicating that Albanese shouldn't speak. He cocked his head slightly as he studied first Albanese, then Coombs. 'Alright. Alright. You're both looking good. You,' he said, gesturing to Albanese, 'are crisp and obviously tasty, and there's demand for your type right now.'

'My type?'

'Yes, you know. The Mediterranean look. Quintessentially Italian.'

'I am Italian.'

'Yes. That's good.' He smiled and turned to Coombs. She let him look her up and down. 'You, on the other hand, I'm not sure. Why the fierce look on such a pretty face? Depends what you've got under that suit. I'd have to see your stills and demo tape. If you have them with you, you can both leave your portfolios with Mrs. LaBette. I'll look them over as soon as I can find more than thirty seconds. Sorry, kids, but that's all the time I can give you now.' He turned toward the two young women but Coombs grabbed his shoulder.

'Here's something you should look at first,'

she said. She held out her badge. 'I'm Detective Coombs. This is Detective Albanese. I'm afraid we need a little more than thirty seconds,' she said. 'And we need it now.'

Orwell looked quickly at Mrs. LaBette, then back at Albanese and Coombs. 'Oh. Dreadfully sorry. I'm not used to having police officers on the premises.'

'Would you like to step into your office?' Albanese said. 'We need to ask you some questions.'

'Do you think that's necessary? I haven't done anything...' Orwell stopped. 'Oh-h-h. Is this about poor Zane's murder? Please tell me that isn't why you're here.'

Albanese nodded. 'I'm afraid it is.'

'Oh my Lord. Are you serious? Well, I don't know anything.'

'We'd like to ask you a few questions, Mr. Orwell. Like, where were you around midnight?'

'Oh shit. Surely you don't think *I* killed the man? I am not a violent person, I assure you. Tell them, Mrs. LaBette. Tell them I'm not a violent person.'

'He's not a violent person,' Mrs. LaBette said.

Albanese smiled and nodded at the receptionist. 'Mr. Orwell, where were you last night around midnight?'

'Where every decent soul should be. Home and in bed.'

'Alone.'

'My, how impertinent.' His smile dropped. 'Yes, alone.'

'Your car was spotted at Kowalski's house a couple of times this last week,' said Coombs. 'Now, if you could tell us what your connection to Mr. Kowalski was, we'd appreciate it.'

'That's simple. I'm a casting director. Zane is ... was ... a producer. I was discussing his upcoming films to see if he could use any of the talent I represent.'

'And did he say if he could use any of your people?' Coombs asked.

Orwell turned slightly to address her. 'A few possibilities, but one most definitely. In fact, we had recently worked out the details for a contract. We were about to sign the deal. It was most likely going to happen today.' He took a puff on his cigarette holder. 'Of course, that isn't going to happen now, is it?'

'Does this person you were about to sign the contract for have a name? And do you have a picture of her – I assume it's a she – by any chance?' Coombs asked.

'Absolutely,' Orwell said. 'Front and center,' he said, pointing at the wall gallery. 'She's that gorgeous redhead in the middle row. She's in demand, you know? Probably the most sought-after star of adult films in this area in the last ten years.' He looked for a sign of recognition.

'I have no idea who that is,' Coombs said.

'Me, neither,' Albanese said.

'Puritans! That is none other than Velma Vixen.' He ran his hand through his hair. 'Mrs. LaBette, could you bring me a folder of Velma's publicity shots, please?'

'Right away, Mr. Orwell.'

'Look, officers, I have to ask you to keep the information I've given you to yourselves, please. With Kowalski dead, the deal is obviously not going to be finalized right away. Maybe it's as dead as he is.' He sighed. 'Sorry. That was inappropriate. Maybe we had better step into my office after all.'

Orwell led them down the hallway to an office filled with movie memorabilia – posters, trophies, awards, photos of actors and actresses from the first silent films to some of the most current silver-screen smashes. Many of the pictures were autographed.

'Close the door, if you please,' Orwell said.

Coombs closed the door. 'We're all ears.'

'I don't know how much you know, but Kowalski was about to become a big player in the adult film industry around here. I'm not sure if his partner, Trey Brightman, will be able to secure the same deal with the distributors or not, but he's walking the walk already.'

'And by that you mean?' Coombs asked.

'He contacted me about Velma's deal. He said he would be willing to renegotiate the deal if we were still interested. I asked if he had inked the deal with the distributor. He said not to worry. Ha.'

'So you doubt that the distributor will take a chance on Brightman?'

'I doubt it indeed but you never know. Of course, if he knew I was speaking with you, it could well put the kibosh on the whole affair anyway.'

'Let me make sure I understand this,' Albanese said. 'Kowalski was about to make his mark in the porn business and was signing top talent. Now, everything is up for grabs again. That about right?'

'That's exactly right,' Orwell said. 'He was already a small-time player. Locals knew him. But, if he could have landed the deal he was telling me about, it would have made him *numero uno*.'

'Was he getting a financial backer?' Coombs asked. 'Do you know who it was?'

'He wasn't getting new money exactly. He was getting a distributor. You can make all the movies you want but if no one handles the distribution, you end up with a basement full of DVDs. He told me he was getting the top guys. I asked him who they were, which group, but he said to hold on for a while and I'd see. I guess it was hush-hush and he didn't want to queer the deal by letting the name out.'

'I see,' Coombs said. 'That makes sense.'

'No problem, but seriously, you have to do everything you can to keep this quiet. If word got out that I was talking to the cops, my position in the industry would be tenuous at best. It's not as if you guys have given the business the easiest of rides.'

'No pun intended?' said Albanese.

'I'm serious,' said Orwell. 'I've seen people blackballed for less. Then what would I do?'

'Used-car salesman?' Coombs said.

'Pimp?' Albanese said.

'Hilarious,' Orwell said. 'You two are so funny. But no one else is laughing. Especially not me. This is serious business.'

Orwell jumped when his receptionist knocked and stepped through the door with a scarlet leather file. 'Yes?'

'You asked for Velma's file.'

'Thanks, honey. That'll be all for now.'

Mrs. LaBette left the room. Orwell handed the folder to Albanese. Coombs peered over his arm.

Albanese slid the sheaf of glossy photos from the file. The first was the same as the headshot on the reception wall, but the second showed Velma lying naked on a sauna bench, her back arched provocatively, red hair cascading over her breasts. Coombs gave the rest of the photos a perfunctory glance. Velma by the pool, Velma on a sheepskin rug by the fire. Jeez, guys were original, weren't they?

'For an old-timer, she looks pretty damn good,' said Albanese.

'Yeah, but if you leak the information I've given you, she might not continue looking that good. See, if Velma's current employer finds out she was trying to bail on him and go to the competition, it could get a little dicey for her. For me, too.'

'Why's that?' Coombs asked.

He took a deep breath. 'If the deal with Kowalski went through, he'd have her as an exclusive. That would take Velma off the market. Other producers would be pissed because I didn't tell them ahead of time and for negotiating such a deal in the first place, especially without letting them make an offer themselves.'

'I see,' Coombs said. 'You think you could give us the names of these other producers?'

'It's a long list. I mean, we are in Hollywood, you know?'

'Why don't you see how many you can come up with?' she said.

'If you insist. I'll ask Mrs. LaBette to bring in our contact list.'

'Can she print us out a copy?'

Orwell picked up the phone, pushed the intercom button and called his receptionist. 'Mrs. LaBette. The *clients* I'm with also need a list of our producers. Could you print them off a copy, please?'

'Certainly.'

'You can pick it upon the way out,' Orwell said, gesturing toward the door.

'We would like to go over that list with you before we leave,' Coombs said.

'Is that really necessary?' Orwell asked. 'I have clients waiting – real ones.'

'It won't take long,' she said. 'Besides, once we check the list, hopefully we won't have to come back. Won't that be nice?'

'Just peachy,' Orwell said, giving a smile that didn't reach his eyes. He sat behind his desk. Coombs sat across from him on a black leather couch, while Albanese wandered about the office, seemingly taking an interest in the various memorabilia. Mrs. LaBette knocked, entered the room and handed the list to Orwell.

'Thank you, my dear,' he said. 'You've been a rock.'

'Mr. Orwell?' Mrs. LaBette said. 'Those two young ladies in the waiting room left. I asked them to leave their portfolios but they said they would rather not.'

Orwell's shoulders dropped an inch. 'Thank you. That will be all,' he said. He offered the list to Coombs.

'That's good, yeah, but what I really need is for you to mark the names of anyone that might have been affected by the Kowalski deal.'

'Affected?'

'Come on, Mr. Orwell, don't play dumb.

Which producers were the ones who would have been pissed about your deal for this Velma Vixen woman?'

Orwell skimmed the list, occasionally placing a checkmark next to a name. He finished and handed the sheet to Coombs.

Albanese stood over her as she looked down the list.

'Shelagh Anders?' she said.

'An ex-star trying to get in on the other end of things,' Orwell said.

'Trey Brightman. No surprise there,' Albanese said.

'Denver Collins. That's who Kahn and Wagner went to see.'

'And then we skip to the bottom,' Albanese said. 'To Teddy Thompson. None of these guys in the middle concerned?'

'Not really,' Orwell said. 'Several guys go under every year – it's not an easy business, you know. Thompson is a small player just like those other guys but with one difference.'

'And that would be?' Coombs asked.

'He didn't sell out.'

'Interesting,' she said.

'Of these four you picked from the list, who had the most to gain from Kowalski's death?'

Orwell put another cigarette into the tortoiseshell holder, lit it and inhaled. 'It would have to be Brightman or Collins,' he said eventually.

'Are either of them the kind that would resort to violence?'

'Both. Brightman is a tough son-of-a-bitch. He used to be a dancer before he was a performer. I don't know that he's ever done anything, you know, like beating somebody up or something, but he sure as hell could whip my ass.'

My grandmother could whip your ass, thought Coombs. 'How about Collins?'

'Now there's somebody that scares the hell out of me,' Orwell said. 'Do I think he could have killed Kowalski? Damn straight he could have. It would not surprise me at all. He wouldn't have done it himself but he sure could have had it done.'

'Okay. Thank you, Mr. Orwell,' Coombs said.

'You're not going to tell Collins what I said are you? He'd be pissed if he found out, and if Brightman doesn't pick up Zane's options, Collins may be the man in charge for a while longer. My people have to work. You see what I'm saying?'

'We understand,' Albanese said. 'We'll do what we can to keep this under wraps.'

He and Coombs left the Yellow Lady Agency. Albanese pulled his driving gloves on before he touched the steering wheel. He started the car, flipped the air conditioner to full blast and lowered the windows to vacate the hot air. 'Do you know what? I feel some sympathy for Mr. Orwell.'

'Why do you say that?'

'He's got his tits in a wringer. At least, he's got his girl's tits in a wringer. He's trying to pick the winner in a winner-take-all situation. If he picks wrong, he's up shit creek.'

'I understand what you're saying. He's no killer. It doesn't make sense to kill a producer. Vixen, on the other hand... This might be a case of a woman scorned. I think we ought to go talk to Velma.'

'I thought we were eliminating women due to the ferocity of the attack.'

'Don't underestimate us,' said Coombs. 'Remember Aileen Wuornos.'

15

Two shots like whipcracks scorched the air and Reyes threw himself behind the jukebox. The sound of screeching chairs and pounding feet filled the bar as the customers fled towards the exits. Reyes fumbled for his gun and radio. Another shot and glass from the jukebox showered down on him. 'Dammit. Shots fired. Assistance needed.'

He peeked around the corner. The crowd was splitting into groups, one rushing toward the front door, one to the side exit. Fontana fired again. Reyes ducked, then leaned out and squeezed off a round at Fontana. A whiskey bottle behind the bar exploded.

'Hang on, Sal!' Wagner screamed through the radio. 'I'm fighting this mob to get in.'

'Same here, same here!' Kahn yelled into the radio.

Fontana rose now from behind the fallen table and fired three shots in rapid succession. The jukebox stopped playing 'Oye Como Va' and pieces of plastic exploded across the room. Reyes curled up against the wall, making himself the smallest target possible.

'I'm almost in,' Kahn said. 'Where are the shooters, Sal? Goddam people, get the fuck outta my way. Police. Let me through. Goddammit. What the...' Another shot.

Reyes pressed his send button. 'Kahn? Kahn, you okay? Shit. Fontana's armed. There's one other shooter. Kahn?'

'What happened?' Wagner asked. 'What the hell happened? I'm almost in. Move it! Move it! Kahn? Reyes, can you see Kahn?'

'No,' Reyes said. 'He was in a crowd by the side door. I'm going to move closer.'

'Stay the fuck where you are,' Wagner ordered. 'I'm almost in. Stay where you are.'

'What the hell is going on in there?' Wallace asked. 'I'm by the side door outside. Where are the shooters?'

'I think Fontana and Tonto are in the pack

coming out now. Careful, Phil. Take cover,' Reyes said. He glanced to his left and saw Wagner stumble into the room. 'Hey, I'm over here,' he waved.

Wagner's eyes met his. His weapon was drawn and pointed downwards. 'Where's the shooter?' he shouted.

Reyes popped up and aimed at the area the shots had come from. All he saw was the back of a few heads and people pushing and shoving to get out. A bullet smacked into the wall behind Wagner's head, and he ducked instinctively, dropping to one knee and raising his gun.

Reyes tried to pick out the shooter but couldn't risk the shot. Whoever had fired was in the pack. He couldn't see either Fontana or Tonto.

The last two men pushed through the door, leaving the bar eerily silent, apart from an upturned glass that splashed beer into a puddle on the floor.

'Phil,' Reyes said into his radio, 'the shooters are outside. Watch their truck.' He crouched behind the remains of the juke-box, his gun still pointed toward the side door. Wagner peered over the bar, gun ready. He lurched back, then placed both hands on the wood and vaulted over.

'Son-of-a-bitch!' Wagner shouted. 'You nearly got your fucking head blown off.'

Reyes ran forward, his gun trained on the

side door. He looked over the bar. The bartender sat on the floor, his empty hands raised. He was as calm as could be, as though he were simply taking a break from work.

Wagner turned toward Reyes. 'Cover this guy,' he said. 'I'm going to check on Kahn.'

Phil's call came over the radio. 'It's a stampede. Could use a little help.'

'Hey,' the bartender said. 'You said you weren't going to bust up my place.'

'If you aren't in jail by three o'clock, consider yourself lucky,' Reyes said. 'I ought to blow your fucking head off myself. It would have gone down peaceful if you hadn't squealed on me, you prick. You almost got me killed.'

'I'm on 'em,' Wallace's voice announced. 'They're heading for the truck. Somebody get the hell out here.'

What a fucking mess!

Reyes rushed to the end of the bar, and saw Kahn. He was lying crumpled on the floor, blood staining his shirt, his head pressed at a sharp angle against the wall. Wagner knelt over his partner, tying to stem the blood flow.

'Move his head off the wall so he can breathe. Get that tie off,' Reyes said. 'Open the top button of his shirt.'

Wagner responded without a word. He gently lowered Kahn's head to the floor, removed the tie and opened his collar. He took the tie and used it as a compress to cover the wound.

Reyes squeezed the button on his radio. 'Ten-two. Officer down. Officer down. Need ambulance at the Mexican Smuggler.'

The response crackled into the smoky air of the bar. 'Ambulance responding.'

'Hang tough,' Reyes said. 'I'm going to help Phil.'

'Get the hell out of here,' Wagner said, his ear to Kahn's mouth. 'Go get the bastards.'

Reyes bolted through the door. Outside, the crowd had pretty much vanished except for a few stragglers hiding behind trees or cars. Two men were disappearing into an alley. Several people were still running. Then to his left he saw Wallace, whose gun was leveled at the stationary gray truck. Tonto was leaning out of the driver's window, holding his own gun. A shot slammed into the wall of the building. 'Motherfucker,' Reyes yelled, and twisted round. Fontana ran across the parking lot, swinging a gun wildly. Another shot missed Reyes by a good two meters. He returned fire, but Fontana was already climbing into the back of the truck.

Wallace fired at the truck. The back window blew out.

Reyes could hear Fontana yelling, 'Get over, get over.'

'Stop,' Reyes shouted again. He fired again, making sure to aim low so the bullet would

148

not fly over the target and hit some civilian. It struck the passenger door near the handle.

A gun popped through the broken back window and fired at Wallace. She dropped to the busted blacktop of the parking lot and for a second Reyes thought she'd been hit, but then she scrambled behind the bonnet of a battered Ford.

The truck jumped forward into the rear bumper of a pimped black and purple Honda.

Reyes saw Wallace fire from a crouched position, three times. The bullets struck the rear of the truck, which reversed hard into the police car parked behind it, then turned right, leaped over the curb and out onto the street. Reyes tracked it with his gun, but it was too risky. *Fuck.*

'You okay, Phil?' Reyes shouted, running over to where Wallace was standing, slouched and breathing heavily.

'I will be when we catch those sons-of-bitches,' she said. 'Let's go.'

Wallace had climbed into their car and started the engine by the time Reyes was on the radio. 'This is Adam Two-Six-Niner. We have a code ninety-nine. We are in pursuit of a gray Toyota Tundra. Californian license "Big Hank".' They screeched out of the parking lot, and Reyes pulled his seat belt across himself. 'Heading west on West Sunset. Two male occupants. First male, Caucasian.

Identified as Henry Fontana. Second male is a Caucasian or Hispanic. Identified only as Tinto or Tonto. Both men are armed. Code Six C. Occupants are wanted in the shooting of a police officer. All units should respond. Exercise extreme caution.'

The gray truck suddenly changed lanes, forcing an oncoming vehicle to brake sharply. It took a left, and Reyes heard the crunch of two cars hitting each other behind them.

'North on Myra toward Prospect. That's north on Myra.' He released the radio button. 'Shit. Phil, Kahn went down. Looked like a chest shot.' Wallace's eyes remained glued to the streets and the gray truck, twenty meters ahead. 'He didn't look good, Phil.' Reyes paused. 'He looked dead.'

'Dammit,' Wallace muttered. She pressed the gas. 'What the hell went down in there?' Then she looked at Reyes. 'You have to shake it off right now. We have a job to do.'

The truck slowed and began to turn, as if it were about to take another right, and Wallace eased over in pursuit. Then, at the last second, the truck veered back onto Winona and accelerated away.

Reyes reloaded his gun. 'I've never wanted to kill anyone before.'

'Sal...'

'Yeah, I know.' He jammed the clip back into his gun, as the gray truck ran a red and threaded onto Prospect.

16

'Suspect heading west on Prospect toward the intersection on Hollywood Boulevard.' Albanese and Coombs recognized Reyes' voice.

'This is Adam two-forty,' Coombs said into the car radio. 'We're coming off the one-oh-one. Were going to try to get ahead and stop the suspects.'

'Proceed with caution,' said the dispatcher. 'Suspects are armed.'

'Roger that,' said Coombs.

Albanese flipped on the lights and siren. He whipped the car over and sped along the outside lane of Hollywood Boulevard.

'God, I can't believe Kahn's been shot,' Coombs said.

At the exit the traffic bunched up, but Albanese was doing a good job of threading a route. Soon they were hurtling down onto Hillhurst. The old feelings Coombs called 'street beat' surged inside her. This is what she missed.

'Suspect is south on North Hoover,' said Reyes.

'Shit, they've changed direction,' said Albanese. They reached the lights at the

Clayton Avenue intersection. The L.A. Fire Department buildings opposite were quiet.

'Make that west on Clayton,' said Reyes.

'We're back on,' said Coombs. They must be heading right this way.'

The lights went green, and red and blues suddenly appeared to their right. The target gray truck skidded out into the road. Albanese floored the gas and aimed the car toward the truck.

'Brace!' he yelled.

Coombs leaned back, put her arm up in front of her face and turned her head.

Their car clipped the truck's front fender, jerking them sideways, then whipped back, crashing hard into the truck. The sound of screaming tires, busting glass and crumpling metal drowned out the sound of their wailing siren. The car lifted slightly off of the ground, then landed hard. Coombs felt herself thrown to the left and her seat belt snapped tight as the air bags burst into her face. A small groan escaped Albanese's lips. Coombs exhaled suddenly, as though she had been hit in the stomach. There was a burning smell – a strange mix of hot oil, rubber and smoke. As the car slid slowly to a stop, her head leaned against the window. Small parts of the disintegrating car were falling onto the street – bouncing, ricocheting – and everywhere a sprinkling of exploded glass shards.

Across the street she saw that the gray

152

truck had gone nose first into the side of a white delivery van. A man was on all fours in the street. Another guy was tugging at him to get up. 'Fontana,' Coombs mumbled.

She looked at her partner, then pushed the air bag down. Blood trickled down his face. 'Go get those sons-of-bitches,' he said.

Three squad cars converged from different directions, as Coombs jammed open the door, her eyes on Fontana. Their man took a panicked look around, abandoned the prone figure, then ran toward the trees by the Fire Department buildings.

Coombs jumped from the damaged police car. Her legs threatened to give way, but she righted herself, ignored the aching muscles and set off in pursuit of the lurching suspect. 'Stop! Police!' she shouted over the screaming sirens, unsure whether he could even hear, but certain in any case that he wouldn't listen. She reached the fallen man, snatched the gun that rested lightly in his limp hand, and slipped it into her pocket. 'Don't move.'

Fontana had limped onto the grass, but Coombs suddenly saw Wallace making for him, with Reyes a few meters behind. Then Fontana turned and fired. Coombs stiffened as Wallace fell behind a parked car.

'Damn,' she said.

'Phil!' Reyes shouted. He lunged behind a tree as a shot from Fontana's gun tore bark above his head.

'Drop it, dirtbag,' Coombs yelled from the street. She had Fontana covered.

Fontana hesitated. He was a good sixty feet away.

'Drop it now,' Coombs said again. 'Or your dick's coming off.' Her heart slammed against her rib cage. Fontana started to turn toward her. The muzzle of his gun came up. Coombs fired.

Fontana spun as a spray of blood erupted from the right side of his waist. He stumbled but didn't go down.

'Bitch!' he wailed. 'You shot me, you fucking bitch!' His hand was unsteady as he fired back.

Coombs knew the drill. Even in the heat of the moment, statistics from the academy rattled in her head. The chances of an untrained shooter hitting her at that distance were close to nil. She dropped to one knee, and fired two more shots in rapid succession. Fontana's body jerked and he fell face-first into the grass.

Coombs saw Reyes come out from behind the tree, his gun pointed at Fontana as he eased toward Wallace. Behind them came a wave of blue uniforms.

She was breathing hard, but her weapon was still raised and pointing at the prone figure. She jogged over, looking for signs of movement. Fontana didn't even twitch. Only when she'd kicked the gun from his hand did she let herself relax. Fontana was most definitely not getting up. Still, she knelt at his side and placed a finger to his carotid. Nothing. Looking behind her, another officer was kneeling on Fontana's accomplice, applying the cuffs.

Over to her right, Reyes had a hand on Wallace's elbow. She was leaning on the bonnet of a car.

'Is she okay?' Coombs shouted.

Reyes waved. 'She's good.'

'Don't talk about me like I'm not here,' Wallace said. 'What about Fontana?'

Coombs shook her head. 'His buddy's in custody, though.'

Wallace brushed herself off and limped forward slowly, bent down and picked up her gun. 'I guess I got lucky twice there. I stepped on something, twisted my ankle, and fell as he fired.'

Coombs nodded. 'Lucky.'

Reyes retrieved Fontana's gun and handed it to one of the uniforms. 'Book this,' he said.

Wallace put her hand on Coombs' shoulder. 'You alright, Joanne?' The use of her Christian name, as much as the sudden physical touch, shook Coombs out of her trance.

'I think so. A little shaky, but okay.'

'Holster your weapon,' Wallace said. 'Relax. You did well.'

'Oh crap!' Coombs said as she slid her gun into her holster. 'Emilio.'

155

She bolted toward the steaming wreck that had been their police car a few moments earlier. Brake fluid and oil dripped onto the tarmac, and glass and fragments of the fender were strewn in the street. Albanese was leaning against the trunk, a first-aid-kit bandage on his head. Two uniformed officers were standing with him.

'Are you okay?' she asked.

'Yeah. I think so. I hit my head on something – the window, I guess. My neck's a little stiff and my chest is bruised, too, but overall, good shape.' He looked at Coombs face. 'You did good, partner. Seriously. That was good work. You'll probably get a commendation for your action today.'

'You're the one who stopped them. I just cleaned up afterward.'

Ambulances arrived. The EMTs checked Albanese's forehead and wounds. 'You need X-rays,' one of the paramedics said. 'You may have a concussion, whiplash, possibly broken ribs.'

'I'm fine,' Albanese said.

Wallace came over from where Fontana's body was being loaded onto a gurney.

'No, you're not,' she said. 'Quit trying to be a tough guy. You know the procedure. Get in that damned ambulance.'

'I think you better come along, too,' a second EMT said to Wallace. 'Looks like you're having leg problems.'

'I'm fine,' she said. 'I twisted my ankle. Just give me an Ace bandage and I'll soak my foot in some Epsom salts tonight.'

Albanese smiled. 'Come on, Phil. You know the procedure.'

'You're an ass, Emilio. Seriously I'm not... The hell with it.' She limped toward the ambulance.

'Coombs and I will meet you there,' Reyes said.

Wallace waved without looking back. She and Albanese climbed into the ambulance. The EMTs pulled the door shut and the ambulance pulled away.

Coombs, still feeling a little dazed, was impressed with the way Reyes took control of the scene. He asked an Officer Townsend to bring Tonto 'or whatever the hell his name is' to the station. Then he turned to Coombs and nodded at the car she had shared with Albanese.

'Considering the condition of your vehicle, perhaps I can give you a ride to the hospital.'

'Yeah. Thanks.' She dropped into the passenger seat and held out her hands. They were shaking.

Reyes climbed behind the wheel.

'That was the first time I've ever shot someone.'

'We all get the shakes after something like that. Don't let it bother you.'

'Did it happen to you? Your first time?'

His eyes dropped from hers and he started the engine.

'Sal?'

'I've never...' He looked over at her. 'I was trying to, you know...'

She put her hand on his and gave it a gentle squeeze. 'Thanks. Let's go check on the troops.'

17

Captain Siley stood alone in the busy hallway of Corona Memorial Hospital. Around him swirled the strange, distant noises of a hospital in action. He watched staff dressed in white, green and purple passing by at various speeds, some wearing stethoscopes, others pushing carts or carrying charts. During his quarter of a century as a policeman, he had been in any number of hospitals, yet they always seemed unfamiliar and alien.

He felt bad for Wagner. The man's partner was fighting for his life and Wagner couldn't even light up to help calm his nerves. He understood the logic behind the hospital's smoking ban but they should at least provide a smoking room so visitors like Wagner

158

didn't have a nicotine fit.

Siley walked into the waiting room. Kahn's partner was looking out of the window, his head resting on a plane of glass. Without turning he said, 'Looks like they're bringing in our guys.'

Captain Siley crossed the waiting room and watched as an EMT crew helped Albanese out of the ambulance and into a wheelchair. Then Wallace was assisted from the ambulance and she, too, was directed toward a wheelchair. *Shit, the whole department is walking wounded.* Wallace pulled her arm away from the nurse.

'Oh-oh,' Wagner said. 'I don't think she wants a ride.'

'She can be stubborn,' Siley said. 'What the hell am I talking about? She is stubborn.'

Coombs and Reyes appeared. Each took one of Wallace's arms and helped her walk. One of the hospital staff pushed Albanese's wheelchair.

'I'm going down to see what's what,' Siley said. 'Why don't you wait here in case the doctors bring word about Kahn? I'll be right back.'

Siley took the elevator down and made his way to the emergency room. Coombs and Reyes were talking with an admissions clerk.

'Hey,' Siley said. 'What happened to Phil and Emilio?'

'Albanese got banged up when his car

159

collided with Fontana's truck,' Reyes said. 'Phil twisted her ankle pursuing Fontana. They're both in the E.R. right now. I don't think Phil is hurt bad. Albanese – I don't know. A nasty knock to the head. The EMTs wanted to check for a possible concussion and broken ribs.' Reyes pursed his lips. 'What about Don?'

'They're looking at him,' Siley said. 'The nurse told us to wait in the ICU on the third floor. They haven't told us much, but it appears that a single shot passed through his lung and exited his back. He looked in pretty bad shape. Lost a lot of blood. The doctor said they would know more after they ran tests. He also hit his head when he fell and may be concussed. The doctor said that is probably why he was unconscious.'

'Where's Wagner?' Reyes asked. 'We had to leave him with Kahn. No cover. Nothing.'

'You did the right thing,' Siley said. 'Wagner's fine. Worried about his partner but otherwise okay. He's upstairs. Who got Fontana?'

'I did,' Coombs said softly. 'Albanese actually stopped him. I kind of made it more permanent. Sorry. That sounded bad.'

'Are you okay?' Siley asked.

'Yeah. My stomach is a bit queasy. It's different from shooting silhouettes on a firing range.'

Siley put his hand on her shoulder. 'Hope

160

that you never get used to it. If you do, quit.'

'She probably saved Wallace's life,' Reyes said. 'Phil was flat on her face and Fontana had her dead in his sights.'

'Make sure that's in your report,' Siley said. 'Tell Wallace to include it, as well.' He stepped over to the admitting nurse. 'Will you send those two officers up to the ICU waiting room when they're done here? Or call us down if they need help.'

'Will do, Captain,' the nurse said.

'Come on, gang,' Siley said. 'Let's go up-stairs and see how our boy is doing.'

When they stepped out of the elevator on the third floor, Wagner was standing in the hall, playing with his cigarette packet.

'Hey, I'm really sorry, man,' Reyes said.

'Me, too,' Coombs said. 'Are you okay?'

Wagner nodded. 'Yeah, thanks. I hear you were a hero today.'

'Hardly,' Coombs said.

'You got the motherfucker that shot Kahn,' Wagner said. 'And his dirtbag buddy.'

'Yeah, well, the crash helped stop them first,' Coombs said. 'Credit Albanese for that bit of fancy driving.'

Siley couldn't remember the last time Wagner went so long without a wisecrack.

A short while later Wallace joined the group. 'Just a mild sprain. I'm fine. Any word on Kahn?'

'No,' Wagner said.

161

'The doctor said they were still checking out Albanese but it didn't appear that he was seriously injured.' She looked at Siley. 'How are you doing, Captain?'

He patted his chest. 'Hanging in there,' he said softly.

'Someone should notify Kahn's girlfriend,' Wallace said. 'Does anybody know her name or where she works?'

'Her name is Angie.' Wagner said. He tapped his finger rapidly against his bottom lip. 'Wait. Con... Angie Cong... No...'

'Do you know where she works?'

'I know that she's a teacher but I don't remember where. Hey. Her number should be in Don's cell phone. Where's his stuff?' He called out to a passing nurse and explained what they needed.

'I'll come with you,' said Siley. 'They may need authorization.'

The nurse led Wagner and Siley to the room where Kahn's possessions had been brought in anticipation of his imminent arrival from E.R. His clothes and personal possessions were in two plastic containers stacked one atop the other. 'Kahn, Donald, Detective' had been written on a piece of white tape and affixed to the lids.

Wagner opened the top one and saw the bloody clothes. 'I should throw this stuff away,' he said. 'Angie doesn't have to see this.'

'Is the phone there?' Siley said.

Wagner set that box aside and opened the other one. On top was Kahn's cell phone. Next to it was a dark blue velvet ring box. Curiosity being an innate trait of good mothers, cats and police officers, he peeked inside. 'What the hell...'

'Wow. That is one pretty ring,' the nurse said. 'I assume your friend is getting engaged?'

'I don't know,' Siley said.

'Not if I can help it,' Wagner said. 'The boy's too young to be getting married.'

'Shame on you,' the nurse said. 'It's none of your business.'

'He's my partner. What the hell does he need a wife for?'

Siley shook his head. That was more like the old Harlen. 'Get his phone and see if the name of the lady he plans on giving that ring to is in there.'

Wagner put the ring back in the box. 'Thanks. Do you have a secure place to hold Mr. Kahn's things? His phone, police ID, the ring are all in here. It needs to be locked up.'

'Absolutely. Here, let me have everything,' said the nurse. 'I'll handle it.'

'I'm taking his phone,' Wagner said. He flipped it open and searched the address book. 'Ah. Here she is. Angie Cunningham.'

The nurse removed the inventory sheet

and had him initial next to cell phone. 'Sorry. I know you're cops, but it's my butt if I don't follow procedure.'

'Everything by the book,' Siley said.

Wagner and Siley returned to the waiting room. 'I don't suppose we've heard anything yet?'

'Not yet,' Wallace said. 'Did you find her name?'

'Yeah. Angie Cunningham. I was wondering, though, should we call her or send a car?'

'Maybe that's more appropriate,' Siley said. 'Call Brooks. Tell him to send a patrol.'

'Thanks,' Wagner said.

'You should have Brooks find out what school she works at,' Wallace advised. 'Have him call the principal. I think it would be better if she knew before the squad car got there. You know, so she can get her stuff together and has a minute to compose herself.' She checked her watch. 'Okay, it's only two-forty. You've still got time. I think they dismiss around three or three-fifteen. Something like that.'

Wagner walked away to make the call.

Wallace, her tightly bound ankle obviously still causing her some pain, walked with Captain Siley to the chairs and sat down.

The Captain was tired and wondered if perhaps Juarez was right. Maybe it was time to reorganize his department. This investigation should have been simple, or at least, not this difficult. He had one cop shot, two injured, the prime suspect killed by a cop, a police car destroyed and, according to Brooks, the owner of the Mexican Smuggler threatening to sue because cops shot up the joint.

Wagner returned to the waiting room. 'Captain, I'd like first shot at Fontana's buddy.'

'No. I don't think that's a good idea,' Siley said. Wagner was wound too tight. That spring might uncoil at any second and it sure as hell couldn't be while he was sitting in the room with one of the guys who shot Kahn. His career, not to mention the department, would be screwed.

'He and Fontana shot my partner. You've got to let me have a go at him. Come on, Chief, I'm not going to kill the guy.'

Siley held Wagner's eye but didn't change his expression. It was too great a risk.

'Captain,' Wagner squatted in front of him, 'I've got to do something. Waiting here is going to drive me crazy.'

Siley looked around the room. 'Okay, I'll tell you what. You take Reyes with you, and by with you, I mean with you every minute, including anytime you are even close to the suspect. And you do everything by the damned book. You got it?'

Wagner rose to his feet. He shot a quick look at Reyes. 'Okay. Someone call me when they come out with word about Don.'

'You have your car?' Reyes asked. 'Or did you come in the ambulance with Kahn?'

'Got mine,' Wagner said. 'Let's go.'

Reyes handed his car keys to Wallace. 'If you feel up to driving...'

'We'll be fine,' Wallace said. 'You'd better catch up with Wagner or you'll be walking back.'

The elevator bell chimed and the doors slid open. Albanese stepped out, with a bandage on his head. He spoke to Wagner and Reyes for a few seconds, then they headed down.

'Hi, Captain,' Albanese said. 'So Reyes and Wagner are going to interrogate the suspect? Who approved that team?'

'I did,' Siley said. 'Probably the final nail in my coffin. So, how are you doing? Everything still in one piece?'

'I'm okay. They said I had a slight concussion and a gash in my head. The doctor said I should go home and take it easy but I told him you'd break my balls if I did.' He smiled.

'You sure? I don't want you passing out or anything.'

'Yeah, almost normal.' He turned to Wallace. 'How about you?'

'Sprained an ankle,' she said. 'They wrapped it and gave me a pain pill, which is what I was going to do on my own. I figure that probably cost a couple of hundred to let them do it.'

'You're worth every penny,' Captain Siley said. 'Okay, let's see what we have here. I think we all agree that Fontana and his crony are probably our guys. I'd like to get some confirmation. Wagner and Reyes are going over to squeeze this Tonto. I need you three to go over and rip up Fontana's place first, then the other guy's.' He looked past them at a tall male in a dark blue suit walking past the windows of the waiting room. 'Phil. Your hubby's here.'

'Uh-oh,' Albanese said.

18

David Wallace strode into the room, and looked about urgently. As he spotted Philippa, he hurried over but stopped a couple of metres short, collected himself.

'You okay, honey?'

She didn't move any closer to her husband. 'I'm fine, just a twisted ankle. Kahn got shot.'

David Wallace sucked a breath through his teeth. 'How's he doing?'

'We're waiting to hear,' said Siley. David Wallace broke his gaze from his wife. 'Captain Siley, detectives...' He nodded to each of them, then faced Coombs. He offered his hand. 'I don't think we've met. David Wallace, Force Investigation Division.'

'Joanne Coombs,' she replied taking his hand. Siley saw her face flush. 'You're here for me, aren't you?'

Wallace put up his hands. 'Why do the FID always get that response? We're on the same side, aren't we?'

'That depends,' said Albanese. 'Why are you here?'

Philippa leaned forward and looked at her husband. 'You didn't come down here to check on me or even us, did you? You're here because of the shooting, right? This is official business, isn't it?'

'Of course I came to check about you first, Phil,' David said. 'But I do have a duty to perform.' He looked at Coombs. 'Detective Coombs, sorry this has to be so formal. Just following procedure, you know.'

'I understand. What do I need to do now?'

'I need to ask you for your weapon and have you accompany me to the station. We'll review the action this afternoon.'

'Action that surely saved my life and other lives, as well,' Philippa said.

'Never the less, it is department regulation that all incidents involving the discharge of a weapon by a police officer must be investigated. Given the resulting fatality in this case, dealing with the incident quickly is imperative. We are also looking into the shooting of Detective Kahn at the Mexican Smuggler. Are the officers involved in that incident here, as well?'

'Only me,' Philippa said.

'Kahn is in surgery,' Siley said. 'Coombs killed the man who put him there. Wagner and Reyes are back at the station interrogating the man who fired on my officers. Officers who all put their lives on the line today.'

'Alright, calm down, people,' said David Wallace. 'I know this is an emotive time for everyone, but we all have a job to do. Phil, I'll come back to you later. Coombs needs to accompany me now.'

'Hold it, David,' Philippa said. 'We're still wrapping up this investigation. Do you need to have Coombs right away? If you can put off the Smuggler investigation, why can't you put off this one, as well? It came about as a direct result of what went down there.'

David Wallace was silent for a moment and looked at the floor. 'I'm sorry, Detective,' he said with a clipped tone. 'It's department procedure. The shooting at the bar did not result in the death of anyone – God willing.'

'Do I need to contact my rep?' Coombs asked as she handed over her weapon. 'Because I don't know who it is.'

'No, you don't need legal help at this time,' he said. 'But how come you don't know who your rep is?'

'It's my first day on the squad.'

'Ouch,' David Wallace said. 'Day one and already in the thick of it, eh?'

'She's not a rookie,' Philippa said. 'She's just new to the squad.'

David Wallace nodded. 'You ready, Detective?'

Coombs nodded then accompanied him toward the elevator.

'That leaves you two,' Siley said. 'My walking wounded. You think you can do the apartments? If not, I can pull Brooks out to lend a hand.'

'We can handle it,' Wallace said. 'Can you drive, Emilio?'

'Hell yes.'

Siley was all alone in the hallway again. The sound of approaching footsteps caused him to turn. A man, maybe Indian or Pakistani, dressed in a doctor's scrubs walked up and introduced himself.

'Good afternoon, sir. I am Doctor Kumar. You are waiting on word about the police officer, Donald Kahn?'

'Yes,' Siley said.

'First, let me assure you that your officer will be fine.'

'Damn, that's good news.'

'Yes,' Dr Kumar said. 'He is not going to be able to go back to work tomorrow, or for a while, but it's good news. We'd some concerns at first that there might be air in the

170

pleural space, or vascular damage. Fortunately, he's remained stable. There's been no evidence of persistent hemopneumothorax...'

'Stop right there, will you, Doc?' Siley said. 'Look, I don't mean to be rude, but I'm not going to follow all that medical mumbo-jumbo. All I really want to know is if Detective Kahn will be alright?'

'Yes. Recovery will take a while, a few weeks probably, but he should be good as new, sooner rather than later.'

'When can I see him?'

'In a little while. He is sleeping very soundly from the anesthesia. He will be brought to this floor momentarily and will remain here for the rest of the day. Sometime tomorrow I will meet with his anesthesiologist and pulmonologist. If recovery is as we expect, we will transfer him from the ICU to the Cardiothoracic Unit. Like I said, probably tomorrow. Maybe in the afternoon.'

'Thanks, Doc. Say, his girlfriend is being brought in. Any trouble with her visiting?'

'Not at all. Of course, he won't awaken any sooner for her than for you.'

'Thanks again, Doc,' Siley said. 'Hell, I need a cigar.'

'There is no smoking on the campus,' Dr. Kumar said, before adding with a smile. 'Besides, smoking is bad for you.'

'Yeah,' Siley said. 'So are bullets.' He took out his cell phone and called Wagner first.

19

'Before you go in there, I think I had better tell you a few things,' Brooks said. 'After all, forewarned is forearmed.'

Reyes looked through the one-way window at the suspect. He could feel Wagner bristling beside him. This was going to be fun. The man he had seen only briefly in the dark and smoky Mexican Smuggler had shaggy, long brown hair. He was slightly overweight, with an unshaven face. Late twenties, Reyes guessed. He had a suture bandage across his left cheek, and his left arm was in a sling.

'He looks a little knocked up,' Reyes said.

Brooks grunted. 'I expect the sling is in preparation for suing the department.'

'Let's do this,' said Wagner, reaching for the door.

'Hold it,' said Brooks. 'Siley said folks high up aren't happy with the way things are going with this investigation so far. If Kahn had not been shot, he said that he'd have everybody's balls or tits nailed to his office door. The Captain's holding off DC Murray, the press and Juarez, but you had better be careful, starting with doing things right in there. He also said that he wants to know who in the hell authorized the charge of the light brigade this afternoon?'

Reyes. looked at Wagner. 'Harlen?'

'Yeah. It was me. Look, can we skip that shit right now. I want to get in there,' he said, gesturing to the interrogation room. 'Time's wasting.'

'The only strike against this guy is for handling stolen goods and possessing a concealed weapon. I don't think you should be using any rubber hoses on him.'

'What's his real name?' Reyes asked.

Brooks handed him the folder. 'Tinto "Tonto" Salinas.'

'You're shittin' me,' Reyes said. 'It's both? Tinto and Tonto?'

'Come on. *Kemo Sabe,*' Wagner said, grabbing the folder. 'Let's go talk to Tonto.'

'Remember,' Brooks said, 'you catch more flies with honey than with vinegar.'

'Yeah, maybe, but I'm out of fucking honey.'

Brooks looked at Reyes. 'Cooler heads need to prevail, Sal.'

Tinto Salinas looked up when Wagner and Reyes walked in. 'You guys have a cigarette? he asked. 'I think I left mine on the table in the Smuggler.'

Reyes held Wagner's shoulder, but Wagner simply nodded. 'It's okay,' he said. 'So, Tonto, where'd you get that faggy nickname? Down Mexico way? You the Lone Ranger's sidekick or something?'

Reyes recognized the procedure – throw the suspect off before firing the real questions. But Wagner was doing it so well he wondered if it was actually for real. He leaned against the window, ready to add the second barrage if necessary.

'Go fuck yourself, man. What does my name have to do with anything?'

'I just like to get to know folks. You know how it is,' Wagner said. He moved slowly behind the seated Salinas, then hit him on the back of his head with an elbow.

'Hey!' Salinas yelled. He looked at Reyes, who immediately turned toward the window and wiped away a phantom piece of dust.

'Do you take drugs, Tonto?' Wagner asked.

'I don't think I should answer that,' Salinas said. 'I think maybe I need to talk to a lawyer.'

'I'm not trying to trap you, Tonto. I was wondering if you ever shot up. I wanted to see how good your veins are. I don't want them to have any problems finding a nice fat vein when they stick the needle in your arm at San Quentin.'

'What the hell are you talking about?'

'Well, let's see. You shot a cop. If he dies...'

'I didn't shoot no cop...'

'You had a gun.'

'But I didn't shoot him.'

'You tried to, and since your buddy

Fontana died in a shoot-out with police, that makes you liable for his death, as well.'

'You're full of it, man.' He pointed at Reyes. 'I didn't know he was a cop.'

'Bullshit,' said Reyes. 'The barman told you, and I identified myself.'

'And of course, there's also poor Mr. Kowalski. You did an awful number on his head. They said there wasn't anything left of his face. Why were you so pissed at him?'

'Who the fuck is Kowalski?'

'So I figure three dead guys in exchange for your worthless carcass is a slam dunk for a jury.'

'Look. Fontana hired me from time to time to help him move stolen shit.' He brought his hands together. 'That's all.'

'That's all?' shouted Wagner. 'Is that what you think? Listen, Tonto, you and Fontana had a shootout with the police less than three hours ago. One of you shot a cop. By law, that means you both shot the cop, no matter who pulled the trigger. Right now you're looking at attempted murder. That's a ten-year stretch right there. If he dies, that's a capital offense all by itself. And if we find a trace of your ass over at Kowalski's, even a hair, we help establish your relationship to his murder, as well, and that means you qualify for a free syringe from the State of California.'

'Look guys, I've got two kids,' Salinas said. 'Their mom is sick. She can't work and she can't take care of them.' He looked at Wagner, then Reyes, who shrugged. 'I can't go to jail. I didn't kill anybody.'

'What can we do?' said Reyes. 'You have to help yourself.'

'How? I didn't shoot anybody. All I know is that you came out of the bathroom firing. Fontana and me, we were just looking out for ourselves, man.' The aggression had left his voice. He was close to cracking. 'Isn't there something you can do?'

'You talking a deal?' said Reyes. 'You're the one that set off that shoot-out at the Smuggler by pulling your gun. You shot a cop. You didn't ask him if he had kids before you shot him, did you?'

'No. No. Wait a minute. I didn't shoot that cop. I pulled a gun, but I didn't shoot no-body.'

'Don't give me that shit. We have your gun and the bullets from the walls of the Smuggler. Some yours, some Fontana's.'

'I didn't shoot him. It was Fontana. I was trying to get the hell out of there. Come on, give me something here. Throw me a rope.'

'Alright,' Wagner said. 'Why don't you tell me what you know about the Kowalski killing, if it helps wrap that case up, I'll per-sonally speak to the D.A. Hell, you might even live to see your kids again.'

There was a knock on the door. A tech-nician entered the room, carrying swabs and plastic bags.

'You say you didn't kill Kowalski right?' Reyes asked.

'Right,' Salinas said. 'I didn't do it. It was obvious that Salinas was looking for a friend – the good cop – and Wagner sure as hell wasn't the one.

'Will you voluntarily surrender a DNA sample? That could go a long way to proving your innocence,' Reyes said.

'Go for it,' Salinas said.

'And you don't want a lawyer first?' Reyes said. 'If you do, the offer is off the table, of course.'

Salinas looked at Wagner, who stood a few feet away, arms folded across his chest. Wagner didn't move – not a twitch, not a breath. Salinas turned back to Reyes. 'I don't want a lawyer Take your sample.'

The technician swabbed the inside of Salinas' mouth. 'Got it,' he said. He walked out and closed the door.

'Can I have a cigarette now?' the suspect whined.

'Sorry. The good folks downtown made it illegal to smoke in public buildings,' Wagner said. 'We don't want to add that to the list of charges against you, do we?'

'Shit,' Salinas said. 'Come on. I'm co-operating. What do you guys want to know?'

'Tell us what went down at Kowalski's house?'

'I wasn't there,' he said. 'Fontana did the burglary. As far as I know, he did it all by himself. Then he called me to help him sell the stuff.'

'Why would he ask you to help him? He knew how to handle that part of his business. I mean, the man took all the risks by breaking and entering. Then he gets to the easy part of selling and decides to cut you in?'

'He was carrying two strikes, man. He wasn't about to go away for good just because he sold some hot cameras to a fence. You know? He was being careful.'

'Apparently not careful enough,' Wagner said. 'We're turning Fontana's apartment right now. Whatever shit hole you live in will be next. You had better be telling us the truth, man, or our deal is off.'

'You won't find anything at my place, I guarantee. I sold some cameras and stereo equipment a few days back. Everything Fontana gave me. I was at the Mexican Smuggler for two reasons. One was to give him his money for the stolen shit that I unloaded, and second was to pick up a computer and some other stuff. I think maybe a scanner or something. I never saw exactly what he had. We were kind of interrupted.'

'Wait a minute,' Reyes said. Wagner looked confused at the sudden interruption but backed off. 'You say you were going to pick up a computer and other stuff, right?'

'Yeah,' Salinas said.

'If everything was stolen on the same night, why didn't he let you fence everything at the same time?'

'I don't know. He didn't say.'

'And you fenced some stereo equipment and cameras a few days ago?'

'Yeah.'

'A couple of days?' Reyes asked again.

'A few. A couple. Sure I'm sure. Two days. Two and half if you want to get technical.'

'You're lying.'

'Bullshit. Why would I lie? I pushed the stuff a couple of days ago.'

'Then do you want to tell me how you managed to sell something a couple of days before the joint was robbed?'

'What the hell you talking about?' Salinas asked. He furtively glanced at Wagner, then back to Reyes.

'Kowalski's house was robbed last night. He was killed last night.' Wagner stabbed his finger on the table in front of Salinas. 'Last freakin' night.'

'I don't know what happened last night,' Salinas said. 'All I know is that Fontana got back from Baltimore this morning. This morning,' he said, imitating Wagner's mannerism. He could sense their uncertainty, and Reyes tried to mask his confusion. 'That's why we were meeting today. Fontana hit Kowalski's place a couple of weeks ago. He told me to hold on to the cameras and stuff for a week or so to cool them off a little, and then pass them. I'm telling you, he ripped Kowalski's joint off almost two weeks ago, not last night.'

20

'Let's go outside,' Reyes said.

Wagner didn't hesitate. 'Sounds good to me. I need a cigarette.'

'Come on, man,' Salinas said. 'Take me outside with you. I really need a smoke. I told you what I know, didn't I?'

'Can't do it, Tonto,' Wagner said. 'You wait here. We'll be right back.'

Reyes and Wagner closed the door on a cursing Salinas.

'What do you make of that?' Wagner asked. 'You think he's lying?'

'I'll tell you in a minute,' Reyes said. 'I have to make a call first.'

'Okay,' Wagner said. He turned to the uniformed officer who was inspecting the noticeboard. 'Keep an eye on the dipstick for a minute, will you, Daley? I'm going for a cigarette.'

'No sweat,' said Daley. 'Hey. Sorry about your partner. I'm glad he's going to be okay.'

'Thanks, man,' Wagner said. He put a cigarette in his mouth and headed for the back door.

Reyes walked to his cubicle. He took out his can of almonds, ate a few, then picked up the phone and called Manuela Cortez. She picked up after four rings.

'*Sí?*'

Reyes spoke to her in Spanish.

'Hello, Mrs. Cortez? This is Detective Reyes. I hope you and Sara are okay.' He paused, but Manuela didn't respond. 'Listen, Mrs. Cortez, I need to ask you one more question. I won't take up much of your time.'

'I've told you everything I know,' she said.

'Don't worry, Mrs. Cortez,' said Reyes. 'I just need to know whether the last time you cleaned, you wiped up some spillage around Mr. Kowalski's bar. Possibly one of the bottles.'

'I always clean very well.'

'I'm sure you do, Mrs. Cortez. So, do you remember cleaning by the bar – on the carpet?'

'I always vacuum there.'

'Yes, Mrs. Cortez but do you remember a stain on the carpet?'

'No,' she replied. 'Mr. Kowalski was normally very tidy. There was no stain – he would have asked me to shampoo it.'

'Are you sure?'

'*Sí*'

'Well, thank you, Mrs. Cortez. You've been very helpful.'

Reyes replaced the phone and rubbed his temples. What the hell was going on? This sure pissed all over their investigation. He needed some fresh air. Outside, Wagner was standing in the shade of a tree. He explained what he'd learnt from Manuela.

'Well,' Wagner said. 'Any ideas?'

'Let's think about it,' Reyes said. 'My first question is, if the burglary really did happen about two weeks ago, why didn't Kowalski report it? There was nothing in any police report about recent activity at his house. No complaints by neighbors. Nothing.'

Wagner exhaled a stream of smoke and sighed. 'And if Tonto is telling the truth and neither he nor Fontana killed Kowalski, who the hell did?'

'I don't know yet. But while we were looking around Kowalski's place this morning, Phil and I found broken glass and what appeared to have been a good-sized spill around the bar. The carpet was all stained in that area.'

'And what, Colombo?'

'I'm getting there. Kowalski was a boozer. His ex-girlfriend – Sadie Monaghan – said he regularly drank a lot but it was always good stuff. He apparently liked to party on the weekends. Okay? So, anyway, the morning we investigate, the bar in the house was totally restocked with new, unopened bottles, except for a bottle or two. The bar in the pool-house was like you'd expect to find at any bar. Some bottles almost empty, some partially so and some almost full.'

'What do you think that means?'

'The bar supply in the house was destroyed and then replaced – and I know when. Or at least, I narrowed it down. Before I came out here, I called Mrs. Cortez. She said the last time she had cleaned the house, or about two weeks ago, there was nothing unusual about the bar area in the house. There was no sign of the stock being destroyed. She never did any big cleanup. So, two weeks ago, the bar was intact.'

'So we are focusing on when the bar was busted up, right?'

'I'm guessing that it happened the night Fontana broke in, or about two weeks ago. Maybe Fontana was looking for something and pulled the bottles from the bar. Hell, maybe he was just clumsy and knocked it over as he was trying to carry out his loot. For that matter, maybe Fontana was being a dickhead and smashed Kowalski's booze to piss him off. We'll probably never know, assuming Tonto is telling us the truth and Fontana pulled the job alone.'

'Okay, I'll bite. Where is that leading us?' Wagner asked. 'I'm not following this shit.'

'The stain in the carpet was dry. The

broken bottles had been swept up but not too well. The area was not cleaned by a pro like Mrs. Cortez and she told me she didn't clean up a bar spill of any size.'

'And? Come on, man, where is this going?' Wagner asked. He lit another cigarette.

'Phil and I had wondered why a house that had a cleaning lady would be so dusty. Then Mrs. Cortez informed us that Kowalski had told her to stop coming two weeks ago. The murder was last night. The robbery was about two weeks ago, like Salinas said. The primary question before us now is, *why* did Kowalski suspend his cleaning service?'

Wagner thought for a moment. Very deliberately, with a slight grin on his face, he said, 'Because of what was stolen?'

'Bingo,' Reyes said. 'For instance, it may have been something Mrs. Cortez would have noticed was missing. Maybe something she might have questioned Kowalski about. Maybe it was something he didn't want to explain to anyone, including her. Shit, I don't know. Maybe it was insurance fraud. We found a bunch of paintings and stuff in an upstairs bedroom closet. Whatever it is, it's right in front of me and I can't see it.'

'Let's go back in,' Wagner said. 'Maybe we can squeeze something else out of Tonto.' He dropped his cigarette and ground it into the earth. 'How does my breath smell?' He exhaled on Reyes.

'Like an ashtray.'

'Perfect,' Wagner grinned.

They went back inside, and Reyes briefed Brooks on what they had discussed outside. 'Are Phil and Emilio still at Fontana's place?'

'As far as I know,' Brooks replied.

'Ask them to check out the liquor stash.'

'I'll make a call. Anything in particular they're looking for?'

'Anything expensive.'

Reyes held open the door to the interrogation room. Daley was sitting with his arms crossed by the side of the table. 'Has our guest behaved himself?'

'Bitch has been whining for a cigarette,' said Daley, placing his hands on his knees and standing up.

As soon as he was out of the room, Wagner strode in and put his face right up to Salinas. 'Sorry we were gone so long,' he said. 'You know how that is, don't you? Sometimes a guy needs a cigarette.'

Salinas gritted his teeth. 'Come on, man. One fucking smoke. I told you what I know. Be a friend.'

'You're not my friend, Tonto,' Wagner said. 'My friend is in the hospital with a bullet in him that you put there.'

'I didn't shoot him,' Salinas said. 'I told you that.' He scratched his arms and licked his lips.

Wagner pulled out his pack of cigarettes

and played with it. He lit his Zippo lighter, extinguished it, then laid it next to the Marlboro pack on the table.

'OK, Tonto, for the last time: why did Fontana kill Kowalski?'

'Shut up, man – I've never even met him.'

Brooks opened the door. 'Guys, can I see you for a minute?'

'We'll be back, Tonto,' Wagner said. He picked up his cigarettes and lighter. 'I think we're getting another smoke break.' He closed the door.

'What's up?' Reyes asked.

'I got a hold of Albanese at Fontana's apartment,' Brooks said. 'They found a computer, a scanner, a box full of DVDs and some other stuff.'

'No shit?' Wagner said. 'That sort of supports our boy Tonto's story.'

'Then I asked them to check his liquor cabinet like you asked, Sal,' Brooks said. 'Want to know what they found there? One full and one almost empty bottle of,' he looked at his notes, 'Rey Sol Anejo.'

'No surprise,' Reyes said. 'Not a common booze by any stretch but it's in both of our hot spots. That's more than a coincidence.'

'I don't get it,' Wagner said. 'What is that stuff? Is it significant?'

'I'd be surprised if you did know what it was. It's tequila. Four hundred dollars a bottle.'

'Something Fontana probably couldn't afford,' Reyes said. 'But Kowalski could.'

'There was a bottle of that stuff sitting on his bar when we went through his house this morning.'

'The guys at Fontana's are bringing in all the computer stuff and the tequila. Hopefully they can find Kowalski's prints on all of the stuff and lock up the theft part of this case. They are going to hit Salinas' place on the way in.'

'Tell them Salinas has kids and a sick wife. Or so he says.'

'Will do,' Brooks said. 'Now, that brings me to point number two. FID has finished with Coombs, but their recommendation, based on an evaluation by their psychologist, is that it would be best for her not to resume duties until tomorrow. She is restricted to desk duty for the rest of the day.'

'That's so much shit,' Reyes said. 'Where is she now?'

'She's on her way,' Brooks said. 'I agree, but what are ya gonna do? Another case of an LAPD SNAFU.'

'They aren't making it any easier on us,' Wagner said. 'Kahn out of commission. Coombs grounded. Wallace and Albanese beat to hell. The only ones still standing are the three of us.'

'There's nothing we can do about it,' Brooks said. 'The captain told me she was in the FBI's tech area working on their computers and such. I'm going to let her attack Kowalski's computer – see if we can get hold of his emails.' He paused. 'It feels like we're grasping at straws, but we can't sit around with our fingers up our asses.'

'Let's go back in and see if Tonto can give us any more,' Wagner said. 'This theft has got to be linked to the murder. How you doing with those porn tapes?'

'I'm too old for that shit,' Brooks said. 'Oh, Wagner. Albanese said the guy in apartment eleven said to tell you thanks from him and his mother for getting rid of Fontana.'

'What? Oh hell. The pearl diver. Ha!'

'What's that all about?' asked Reyes, holding open the door to the interrogation room.

'Nothing.'

Reyes closed the door and took a seat across from Tinto 'Tonto' Salinas. 'Tonto, my man, you look a mess. Hey, how would you like a shot of tequila? I talked to the boss while we were having a smoke. He said we can't let you have a cigarette but maybe you'd like a shot?'

'Tequila? Oh, man, no way,' Salinas said. 'That stuff is deadly. I don't know how Fontana drank that shit. I'll take a beer, though.'

'Fontana liked tequila, did he?' Wagner said. 'Did he drink the good shit or what?'

'I don't know. Maybe the bartender at the Smuggler can tell you. I don't think they serve anything expensive at that place, though.'

'Mr. Salinas,' Reyes said. 'Do you know why Fontana chose Kowalski's house to break into? Weren't there homes with better stuff to rip off?'

'Yeah. Yeah, I do know why.'

'Well?' Reyes said. 'You want to tell us?'

'Give me a cigarette and I'll tell you. You can keep the beer.'

Wagner threw the pack of Marlboros on the table. 'Okay, let's hear what you've got.'

'Oh no. No, sir. Give me your lighter. If I spill my guts now, you let me keep the cigarette but you don't let me light it.'

'You wouldn't want us to break the law, would you?' Wagner asked.

'Quit the bullshit. Give me the lighter.'

Wagner shot Reyes a look, and slid his Zippo across the table. Salinas lit his cigarette, exhaled and sighed.

'Come on,' Wagner said. 'And it had better be good or I'll put that damn thing out on your forehead.'

Salinas took another drag. 'Okay. Here it is. Fontana told me that some rich dude over in Calabasas wanted something from Kowalski's computer. Fontana said they wanted CDs or DVDs or something but no matter what else he found, he was supposed to take the computer tower because the guy wanted the hard drive or the information off of it.'

189

'Do you know who this rich dude in Calabasas is?' Reyes asked, although he could guess.

'No. I swear to God I don't know. That's what Kowalski called him – "the rich dude over in Calabasas".' He drew deeply on the cigarette.

'You better not be shitting us,' said Wagner.

'I wouldn't,' said Salinas, settling back in his seat. 'He was heading out of town. Henry passed me the cameras and stuff he wanted to dump, and asked me to drop something in the mail for him. It felt like a DVD.'

'Who to?'

'I can't remember,' said Salinas. 'It was some office unit in Burbank.'

'We need a name,' said Reyes.

'I can't remember. I wasn't interested in Henry's mail, was I?'

'Come on,' Reyes said. 'Let's go.'

Wagner walked toward the door. 'Somebody will be in for you in a minute,' he said. 'You'd better enjoy the cigarette, Tonto. It might be your last one for a long time.'

Wagner and Reyes left the room and closed the door. Brooks was waiting. 'That sounds an awful lot like Denver Collins to me.'

'No,' Wagner said. 'It sounds exactly like Denver Collins the second.'

'I don't get it,' Brooks said.

'It's nothing. You had to be there.'

21

'I told you there was nothing to worry about,' Brooks said. 'FID always come on strong at first. They're just covering their own asses.'

Coombs leaned back from the keyboard. It was almost four o'clock, but still baking outside, and the desk-fan was working overtime, blasting her face with cool air. 'Yeah, it's all okay as far as I know. They said I could resume regular duties in the morning.'

'That's good.'

'I did get a laugh out of some of their observations,' she said. 'One of the FID guys asked me if I knew that Fontana's gun was empty of cartridges when he went down. I said, "Hell yes, it was empty. He was shooting at cops with it." He said they would have to confirm that and then they could close the books on the investigation.'

'Jesus. Hey, I know you'd like to go home some time today so let me get the hell out of your hair so that you can figure out if there's anything of interest on that computer.'

'Okay,' she said, and resumed searching Kowalski's files.

Brooks walked down the aisle between the

cubicles. She could hear him talking to Wallace.

'How's that ankle?'

'Not as much of a pain as my husband,' she replied.

Coombs blocked out their conversation. Kowalski was a guy who liked order. A cursory glance over his documents and folders showed everything neatly labeled. The most recent files were dated just over two weeks ago, to be expected if Fontana's buddy wasn't bullshitting them. She opened up his email program.

'Anything of interest?' Reyes said from behind her. He was standing awkwardly, as though he didn't know whether to sit down or not.

'Hi, Sal. What's up?'

'Nothing much. I've been following up the leads you and Emilio got from Orwell – those producers. Turns out Shelagh Anders was up in Anaheim at the wake of her mother, and Teddy Thompson was filming across the state.'

'Did they turn anything at Salinas' place?'

'No. Scared the hell out of his wife and kids, I guess. Did you find anything on the computer yet?'

'Not much but I barely got started.' She scrolled down through Kowalski's recent emails. Several seemed to be from his lawyer, to do with percentages and royalties. Then, seventeen days ago, there was a string of messages from a man called Jacques Brasille at a company called CatwalkG. Coombs read the most recent.

Zane, thanks for coming up here Friday. I know my associates were glad to put a face to the name. Let's proceed along the lines we discussed, and I'll get the legals my end working on something formal. All best, JB.

Coombs scanned the messages from Kowalski that preceded Brasille's email. It was odd, hearing his voice from beyond the grave.

Dear Mr. Brasille, I'm looking forward to discussing options on Friday. I should be at your offices by 2p.m. Still talking with a few agents, but once this is tied up, the best will be knocking at our door. See you Friday. Zane Kowalski.

'Hey,' Coombs said to Reyes. 'Get the Sarge over here. This might be something.'
'Hey, Ray,' Reyes yelled.
Brooks came over, and stood beside Reyes.
Coombs carried on through the chain, which contained boring material about organizing parking at the CatwalkG offices and the timings of the meetings, mostly conveyed through Brasille's personal assistant, a woman called Cyndi Waters. Then Coombs reached the beginning of the correspond-

ence, from Jacques Brasille to Kowalski, some two months before.

First of all, Mr. Kowalski, please don't refer to me as your 'amigo'. I'm a businessman, and this is business, not 'putting things together'. I'm not interested in your petty squabbles with rivals, either. I don't have to tell you that all preliminaries are to be treated with the strictest confidence. Saying that, it was interesting to meet you also, and your proposition had some merit. Please direct further communications via my PA, who is copied above, to fix up a meeting. Yours sincerely, Jacques Brasille.

'Did you find something?' said Brooks. He was holding a polystyrene coffee cup, and there were some crumbs on the front of his brown tie. Coombs read the first email.

Hey, amigo, good to catch up last night, and I'm glad you liked my stuff. Let's put something together asap. Collins will shit his pants. Call me, Zane.

'Albanese and I were talking to Orwell earlier today,' said Coombs. 'He said that Kowalski was making a deal with a big porn distributor but he didn't know which one.'
'And?' Brooks said. 'What did you find?'
'A batch of emails between Kowalski and this guy, who calls himself VP of Talent at

194

CatwalkG Films, a distributor. It kind of supports what Orwell said. It also puts an interesting light on a comment Collins made to Wagner and Kahn. Remember, Collins said he confronted Kowalski and that he backed off so all was right with the world? Now, I haven't read all of the emails yet, but there is every indication so far that the distributor was CatwalkG and that they were going to back Kowalski's film business after all and drop Collins.'

'So Collins was lying. Knock me over with a feather,' Brooks said. 'Sal, get on your computer and check out this CatwalkG Productions.'

'I'm on it,' Reyes said. He walked back to his desk.

Coombs could hear a slight buzz as the other detectives began asking what was going on. Albanese leaned on the wall of her cubicle. 'You have it figured out, partner?'

'Ha. Not quite.'

'Need coffee or anything?'

'Thanks. I'll take a Diet Pepsi if you're buying.'

'Be right back.'

Ten more minutes of reading and a clearer picture was beginning to form in Coombs' mind.

'Everyone listen up,' Brooks said. 'Okay, Sal. What did you find about CatwalkG Productions?'

'They are an up-and-coming distributor,' Reyes said. 'Two companies, Catwalk and G-Spot, merged about a year ago. They started quietly sucking up a lot of smaller producers' products, like Collins'. Once they did that, it forced companies to grow to meet the demand. Smaller competitors were finding it hard. It became a survival of the fittest on both sides of the aisle. Till now, the big winner appears to have been Collins – apparently they signed a deal worth eight million dollars about twelve months ago.'

'Couldn't CatwalkG just buy films from both of the guys?' Albanese asked.

'It doesn't work that way,' Wagner said. 'It's like a guy selling Fords and Chevys. Plus, one guy usually sews up the talent – at least, the big-name talent – and word gets out who the big player is.'

'Always nice to hear from an expert,' Reyes said.

'So Collins stood to lose a bundle,' Albanese said. 'And Kowalski was in line to pick up the same bundle and grow his business. We also found out that Kowalski was trying to hire an actress by the name of Velma Vixen, who was one of Collins' prime assets. She is starting to get long in the tooth but her name still sells movies.'

'But it was the distributor who was pushing for that,' Coombs said. 'Kowalski's emails keep talking about signing up talent.'

'This Velma must have some talent,' Reyes said.

Albanese chucked an envelope toward Reyes, who caught it clumsily. 'What's this?'

'That's the talent,' said Albanese.

Reyes took out the pictures Orwell had given Albanese and Coombs earlier. 'Well, I'll be damned.'

'Huh? said Albanese.

'Phil, take a look at this picture.' Wallace limped over, and Reyes held out the shot of Velma Vixen on the sauna bench. 'Isn't that the woman who beaned our boy Brightman in the massage parlor?'

Wallace took the shot and turned it around ninety degrees. 'I only saw her vertical, but yeah, no doubt. She wasn't calling herself Vixen though. It was Vera Yelland.'

'Velma Vixen must be a stage name,' Wagner said.

'Either that,' Reyes said. 'Or she's got an identical twin.'

'Now *that* I would remember,' Wagner said.

Coombs was already fed up with Wagner's wisecracks. 'So whatever her name is, Velma or Vera, she hits guys in the head with her high-heel shoe when she gets pissed?'

'Only guys in the porn business apparently,' Reyes said. 'Kinky, huh?'

'So have we confirmed that she smacked both Brightman and Collins?' Wallace asked.

'Brightman, for sure,' Reyes said. 'Though

he wouldn't press charges.'

'What did St. Regis say when you called them about Collins' alibi?' Albanese asked. 'Did he have a concussion like he claimed?'

'Collins was bandaged up for innocent reasons,' Brooks said. 'His alibi at St. Regis checked out – some kind of cosmetic surgery done a week ago. Last night he was back claiming that he had fallen and tore some stitches.'

'No shoe attack?' Albanese asked

'The doctor said Collins claimed he ran into the corner of a door.'

'Is it just me or is the center of the problem here this Velma broad?' Coombs asked. 'People are covering for her.'

'Is anyone involved in this case telling us the truth about anything?' Albanese said. 'Dammit, I'm going to call Orwell and get some answers.'

'This ought to be good,' Coombs said from her cubicle. She popped up and walked back to Albanese's desk. 'Put it on the speaker. This Orwell guy's a trip.'

Albanese checked his notes and dialed.

'Jermaine Orwell speaking.'

'Orwell, this is Detective Albanese. From this morning.'

'Detective. I told you everything I knew.'

'Yeah, well, I need a little more specific info. For instance, why did Velma Vixen, or Vera Yelland as her parents knew her, assault

Trey Brightman this morning?'

'What? Damn her. Did she really do that? I told her to let me handle Brightman.'

'What were you going to do, hit him with your shoe instead?'

'Your sense of humor still evades me, Detective.'

'Last chance, Orwell, unless you want to be known across L.A. as a pal to the cops. Why did she attack Brightman?'

Coombs heard a defeated sigh. 'Isn't it obvious, Detective? He wasn't going to honor the deal Kowalski had negotiated. Velma already had an eye on retirement, closing her legs for good. This deal would have sealed it.'

'So she didn't end up signing with Brightman?'

'I told you, nothing was signed. In fact, she is on her way to Collins' place right now. He called and invited her to come over. She said she was going to pretend nothing had happened. You know, no harm, no foul.'

'I'm not sure Kowalski would agree with that analysis.'

'Very droll, Detective.'

'There is also a possibility that Collins knows about your plans,' Albanese said, 'and hers for that matter. Velma could be in for a most unpleasant surprise.'

'What are you talking about? How could he know?' Orwell snapped. 'Oh my God. If Collins knows, there will be hell to pay.'

'Call her on her cell and tell her not to go.'

'I can't. Her phone was dying when she called me. The dumb bitch never charges it.'

'We'll see what we can do,' Albanese said. He hung up and looked at the rest of the detectives. 'We'd better get out there or Velma's phone may not be the only thing to die.'

22

Two minutes later Reyes was checking his clip and was ready to go.

'Sal,' Wallace said. 'I talked to the Captain. He's okay with you staying here at the station.'

'Why would I stay here? Aren't we going to pick up Collins?'

'Yeah, but we don't need everybody. You stay. When we have him in custody, I'll call and you get the hell out of here and go see Fernando. I'd let you go now but sure as shit if I do, something will go wrong and we'd both get in trouble.'

'I don't know, Phil. That doesn't seem right. The other guys aren't getting a break.' Reyes could hear the tone in his own voice and he didn't like it. He wanted to be there when they picked up Collins.

'Trust me on this one. They understand. If

we need you, I'll call. Only this time if I do, come without that yellow suit. Hey, I gotta run,' Wallace said as she headed for the stairs where Wagner and Albanese waited.

Reyes watched her leave with mixed emotions. Sure, he wanted to get over to pick up Fernando. Pam's words thudded in his bead. *He needs structure. Routine. With your job, you can't provide that.* The worst thing about it, she was right. The poor kid had to be confused by everything. Not showing up for his birthday again would only serve to support his ex's bullshit.

He checked his watch. It was 4:15 p.m. It was going to be close. Coombs was still sitting at the keyboard, scanning emails. *She must be itching to be out there, too.* 'What do you want us to do, Ray?' he said to Brooks.

'Coombs can keep searching Kowalski's computer and see what else might be in there. You get a hold of the lab boys and see if they can give us anything on the physical evidence they collected. Then call Doctor Hackett and see what he has. They're all going to bitch and moan about us rushing them but we need answers. Once we have Collins in custody, we'll throw the lot at him till he confesses. You can also help me field calls. If any come in from the papers or news channels, let me talk to them. I can bore the ass off a reporter. And why don't you give that Jacques Brasille a call, as well.

Leave no stone unturned.'

'Okay, will do,' Reyes said.

'Considering the kind of people we're dealing with, turning over stones is probably going to reveal a lot of slimy bastards,' said Coombs.

Reyes ran a check on Jacques Brasille. A few traffic citations was all he found. *I've seen priests with more in their files than this guy,* he thought. Reyes called the listed number for CatwalkG.

'CatwalkG,' a very sexy voice said. 'Cyndi speaking. How may I help you today?'

This is Detective Reyes of LAPD Hollywood Precinct. I would like to speak with Jacques Brasille.'

'I'll connect you,' she said. 'Please hold.'

A minute or so passed. Reyes hummed along with the music playing through the phone until it was cut off by a man's voice with a French accent that could have been faked. 'Jacques Brasille.'

'This is Detective Reyes. I'm investigating the murder of Zane Kowalski. I'd appreciate it if you could answer a few questions for me.'

'I think you have the wrong man, Detective. I don't know anything about his murder.'

'How about you let me ask the questions before you evade them. I understand you and he were negotiating a contract regarding the distribution of his films. Is that correct?'

'I don't mean to be rude. Detective, but I

think it would be better if you spoke with one of our attorneys. I'll get Cyndi back on the line and she'll connect you.'

'Thanks for your cooperation, Mr. Brasille. May I confirm one thing with you before you switch me back to your secretary?'

'And that would be?'

'Your address. See, I need to know what address to put on the search warrant when I send the SWAT team out there today. Oh, and tomorrow. And I think, maybe the day after that.'

'That sounds like a threat. Maybe harassment.'

'No. You've got me all wrong. I'm trying to help you out. Seriously now, with one of your own getting chopped up sometime last night, the spotlight is on all of you.'

'But I had nothing to do with it.'

'Sure, that's probably true but everyone says that. Did I mention that we found your name on the dead man's computer?'

'Okay, okay, okay, okay,' Brasille said. 'I can see where this is going. What do you want from me?'

'Easy one to start. Where were you between, say, midnight and 2:00 am?'

'I was in Dallas yesterday. My red-eye arrived at LAX at five-thirty – fifteen minutes late, by the way.'

'Were you – and by you I mean CatwalkG – negotiating a deal with Zane Kowalski or

Denver Collins to provide films for your distribution company?'

'Detective Reyes, this will of course remain confidential. We told Kowalski that if he could get certain stars under his wing, we'd sign a contract.'

'Velma Vixen?'

The other man was silent for a second. 'Yes, that's right,' he said eventually. 'I spoke with Mr. Kowalski two days ago, and he had seven of the ten names signed up. Miss Vixen is a particularly important asset and she was going to sign within forty-eight hours, by today, in fact.'

'Good,' said Reyes. 'See how easy it is when you try. And once Kowalski was kaput, were you willing to deal with his partner, Trey Brightman?'

'There's no reason in principle why not but, because we weren't sure of the legal status of Big Z Productions – that's what Kowalski was calling his company – nothing has been formalized. Even we are willing to honor the appropriate moratorium for grieving, Detective. If the stars' contracts are with Big Z Productions, and if they are still legally bound to the company despite Kowalski's demise, then we might still consider going ahead with the project.'

'So you might have dealt with Brightman then?'

'Possibly. If he had the stars we wanted...'

'But you weren't ruling out re-upping with Collins' outfit, either?'

'We hadn't discussed it. Like I said, it was a fluid situation.'

'Okay. Thanks.'

Reyes hung up and called the ME's office. Dr. Hackett laughed. 'One of us is psychic. I was just sitting down to call you guys. The hard copy is coming over but here's the bottom line. The vic died somewhere between midnight and two. A little fudge on the time but not much.'

'Cause?'

'The man was clubbed to death with a heavy piece of wood. It was probably shaped something like a baseball bat but it wasn't a bat. The splinters in his skull and under the counter were the same kind of wood – teak. I don't know anyone who makes a teak baseball bat. Something that looked like that, though. A dowel rod maybe? Anyway, you get the general idea.'

'Or a piece of furniture?'

'Sure. There were wounds on other parts of his body but most of those were either defensive wounds, or a swing and a miss by his attacker. The one exception was that someone took care to let him have a few good hits to his crotch.'

'You're saying the guy intentionally beat Kowalski's nuts?'

'Indeed.'

Reyes made some notes and thanked Dr. Hackett Then he hung up and opened his phone list to find his contact in the forensics lab. *Nazer, Sean.* Did they have results on the prints they had not been able to identify earlier?

'We found a bunch,' Nazer said. 'We've identified a few. You already know about Fontana. I hear you guys got him. Good job. How is Kahn doing?'

'He's going to be okay. Thanks.'

'Tell him I said I hope he gets better soon.'

'Will do.'

The technician read the list of the fingerprints that they had identified. Reyes recognized several of the names as he wrote them down, including Jermaine Orwell and Vera Yelland. After he finished, he quickly scanned the list. Obvious by their absence were the names of Manuela Cortez and Tinto Salinas.

'Run a name through your system for me, will you?' Reyes asked. 'Tinto Salinas.'

A minute or two later came the response, 'He's in the system.'

'Run one more, will you? Manuela Cortez.'

Another couple of minutes passed. 'There are several – do you have an address?' Reyes took out his notebook and found the page. 'Silver Lake Boulevard. Number fifteen-fifteen.'

'There's nothing at that address,' Nazer

said. 'Oh and we checked the partial bloody footprints found in the kitchen and hall. Some sort of workboot or outdoor shoe. There are several possible brands it could have come from. You could get any of them at a discount or large box store. Nothing unique. About the only way to positively identify it would be to have the boot that made the print and check for blood. The handprint was made with a glove but way too smeared to ID it.'

Reyes thanked the technician and hung up. He returned to Coombs' cubicle.

Brooks looked up. 'Anything?'

'Our boy Salinas might be telling the truth. They found and identified Fontana's prints about as fast as humanly possible, but there was nothing on Salinas. Unsurprisingly, Manuela Cortez isn't in the system, either.'

'If she's an illegal, there wouldn't be any official documentation,' Coombs said.

'I think we have our man in Collins,' Brooks said.

Reyes nodded. 'I agree, except I think he hired muscle to do the actual killing.' He explained about the wood splinters and bloody footprints and what Dr. Hackett said about the battering of the victim.

'I'm going to go get some of the backed-up crap done while we wait to finish this sucker,' Brooks said. 'Why don't you lend Joanne a hand?'

'I think I can handle that.'

Brooks got up and straightened his back. 'Getting stiff.' He slowly walked back to his desk.

Reyes stood by Coombs' desk for a minute before he spoke. 'How are you doing?'

'Pretty good,' she said. 'The only thing I still haven't figured out is his password. He has something locked up. I'll get it, though. I was pretty good at breaking codes at the FBI.'

'That's good, but I meant how are you doing? You know, in general.'

'It's been a pretty crappy first day back,' she said. Now they were alone, the squad-room was eerily silent. Reyes noticed that Coombs' eyes were glued to the screen. He couldn't blame her – it'd been a long time.

'No shit.' He took a seat. 'But – I meant – how have you been doing since you left for the FBI?'

Oh.' She paused and looked at Reyes. 'I've been doing okay. The FBI was great but it wasn't for me. I missed being in the main-stream, out in the street, doing the day-to-day stuff.'

Reyes nodded. 'I heard about your parents. I sent a card.'

Coombs stopped typing and turned to look at him. Damn, she was beautiful.

'I got it. Thanks. I still can't believe they're gone.'

Reyes wished that the two of them were someplace else. This was neither the time nor the place. The silence was uncomfortable.

'So, how have you been?' she asked him.

'Alight, I guess. Pam divorced me a few years ago. Her dad was so happy I thought he'd have a stroke. He sent a team of lawyers after me and that was that. I didn't have a dime, no home. Nothing.'

'How'd he manage to take your house?'

'He bought it for us when we got married, but he owned it.'

Brooks walked back in, breaking up the brief reunion. 'I have no idea why the media is so hot to trot about this case, but they want every little detail. Hell, I think I gave the last guy my wife's brownie recipe. Anything else on the computer?'

Coombs laughed. 'There are some password-protected files on here. Hopefully it will take only a few more minutes to circumvent the security system.'

'Let me know,' Brooks said. The phone rang. 'I'm going to grab it here. Hollywood Precinct. This is Detective Brooks. Oh. Hello. Just a minute. I'm going to put you on hold.' Brooks pushed the mute button. 'Sal. It's for you. The ex.'

'Fuck, not now.' Reyes returned to his desk and pushed the flashing button. 'Hello.'

'You haven't forgotten, have you? You're still coming to get Nando, aren't you?'

209

Reyes felt his gut tighten when he heard Pam's voice. 'I'll be there,' he said. 'We're wrapping up the case right now.'

'I wanted to make sure. You didn't show up last year for his birthday and you nearly broke his heart. He doesn't know what a jerk you are. He just knows you're his daddy.'

'Listen, Pam, it's been a lousy day. Cool it. I'll be there.' He checked his watch. It was less than a half an hour before he was supposed to pick up Nando. He needed thirty minutes to get to the Vander Bosch estate. Of course, with the sirens he could do it in less.

'When didn't you have a lousy day?' she said. 'That's the reason we got a divorce.'

'No,' he said, lowering his voice and letting his anger hiss. 'No. We got divorced because you were fucking David Nowitzski and probably a dozen other of your daddy's toadies. We got divorced because you loved a whole lot of guys more than me, including your daddy and his money. Especially the money.'

'I'll see you later,' she said stiffly, and hung up.

He put the phone back in its cradle. Nothing he did for Nando would ever be good enough in Pam's eyes. Still, at least he had bought a decent gift. Then a sinking feeling nailed him – the bike. 'Aw, shit!'

Brooks stood up and looked over the top of the cubicle walls. 'Something wrong?'

'Yes, there's something wrong. My son's birthday present is in the car.'

'And?'

'And it's on its way to Calabasas.'

23

Wagner screeched on the brakes in front of Collins' place, making Wallace put a hand on the dashboard.

'Do you always drive this badly?' she said.

'Only when Don's not here to tell me off,' said Wagner.

Albanese was right behind them in a second car.

'We do this by the book,' said Wallace, but Wagner acted as though he hadn't heard her. He was already out of the door.

A pale blue Corvette was parked by a black Mercedes. From the bunny rabbit on the dashboard, Wallace guessed it belonged to Yelland/Vixen.

'I'll take the back,' said Wagner, a grin twisting his lips. 'Please God, let him resist.'

'By the book,' Wallace said. 'We don't want any more shooting today.'

As Wagner crunched off across the gravel. Wallace walked gingerly to the front door with Albanese and rang the doorbell. The

211

theme from *Chorus Line* filled the afternoon air.

'What the hell is that?' Wallace said. She shifted her weight.

'Ankle still hurting?' Albanese said.

'Hell yeah. I even let Wagner drive. That's how sore it is.'

A small, white male with a bandaged head and large ears opened the door. Behind him stood a much larger man, a Pacific Islander by the looks of him, dressed in a black tuxedo.

'Can I help you?' the smaller of the two men said.

'I'm Detective Wallace,' she said, and held out her ID. 'This is Detective Albanese. We'd like to speak to Denver Collins.'

'I'm Denver Collins – the second,' he said. 'What can I do for you?'

'May we come in?' Wallace asked. Albanese was already moving forward.

'The police were here earlier,' Collins said, but he was stepping back, easing the large man back with him.

'Yes, we know,' Wallace said. 'But we need to talk with you and possibly one of your guests.'

'One of my guests?' Collins asked. 'Who are you looking for?'

'Velma Vixen. Is she here by any chance?'

'Velma. Why the hell do you want to see Velma?'

Albanese put his hand on Collins' shoulder. 'Please turn around. I need to check you for weapons.'

'What...'

Albanese spun Collins. The massive body-guard stepped forward. Wallace pulled her weapon and pointed it at him. 'Hold it.'

'Turn around,' Albanese said. He frisked both men. 'Ah. Odd Job here has a nasty pineapple-slicer.' He held up curved-blade knife and laid it on a table. 'We'll just leave that out here.' He took the man's wallet and handed it to Wallace. The driver's license read Keali'i Keiaho. Albanese pulled on Keiaho's shoulder and turned him back around. 'You the guy who played for the Raiders a few years back? Tsunami they called you.'

'That's me.'

'Your career has gone downhill, Tsunami. I hope you haven't done anything stupid here. Why don't you take us to Miss Vixen?'

'Okay,' Keiaho said. 'But I've done nothing wrong. I'm his bodyguard is all.'

'Wait a minute. What the hell is going on?' Collins said. 'Why all the interest in Velma? I believe you guys need a search warrant.'

Wallace pulled out an arrest warrant. 'Will this do?'

'Okay. So what do you want?'

'We need to see Velma now.'

'This is ridiculous. I didn't do anything. And the lady you're looking for is outside by the pool,' Collins said. 'That way.' He pointed toward the back of the house.

'Why don't you both go ahead and show us?' Wallace said.

Collins turned and headed across the hall.

'You, too, Tsunami,' Albanese said to the hulking bodyguard. 'We'll follow you.'

'Let's go through the sunroom. It's a shortcut,' Collins said.

Keiaho opened the door A blast of humid air greeted the visitors. The sunroom was crowded with tropical plants, from small Venus flytraps to large palms and the ever-present bougainvillea. Butterflies flitted through the steamy air. Overhead, a few rare birds chattered and chirped. Wallace closed the door behind them and followed the others to the pool door, her gun in her hand. She didn't feel comfortable and hung back. If something went down, she was ready. Again Keiaho opened the door and stepped outside, followed by Collins and the detectives.

'What the hell...' Collins said.

'What took you so long?' Wagner asked. He sat on a deck chair, a cigarette in one hand, his gun in the other. Next to him was a redhead dressed in a white thong swimsuit. She was reclining on a chaise lounge, a cocktail glass cuddled in both hands.

'You okay, Vera?' Wallace asked.

'Safe and sound,' Wagner said.

Velma took a sip of her cocktail and smiled

coyly. 'Is all this fuss over little old me?'

'Hey, I recognize you,' Collins said to Wagner. 'You're the boor who came to my house, drank my libations and then insulted me. Why are you all so interested in Velma?'

'In a minute,' Wallace said. 'But I will tell you why we were worried about the little lady. A short while ago, the individual that carried out the burglary for you and his partner were arrested. Perhaps you know their names – "Big Hank" Fontana and Tinto Salinas?'

'You know what, officer? I think I had better call my attorney.'

'Sure,' Albanese said. 'But first, see if this sounds familiar. You have the right to remain silent...'

'You're arresting me?'

Wallace nodded. 'That warrant I showed you is a warrant for your arrest, Mr. Collins. You're going to be charged with burglary and conspiracy to commit a burglary, and maybe we can find a way to get Kowalski's murder thrown in there, as well.'

'Murder?' Keiaho said. 'Hey. I didn't know anything about any of this stuff.'

'Shut up, Tsunami,' Collins said. 'Okay, officer, wait a minute now. Listen. What I did was completely legal. It was nothing more than, you know, corporate spying. The big companies do it all the time.'

'Call it what you want, it's burglary,'

Wallace said. 'Now keep your hands where I can see them.'

Collins held up his hands. 'I'm admitting that I was involved but it isn't a crime. That piece of shit Kowalski was trying to ruin my business. Behind my back! I couldn't just sit here and let him do whatever the hell he wanted, could I?'

'So you killed him?'

'Killed him?' Collins said. 'Killed him? We're talking corporate espionage. I was looking for a commercial advantage, nothing more. I was nowhere near Kowalski's when he was killed. Hey, hey,' he said as Albanese started cuffing him. 'Wait a minute. I have an alibi. What's your name? You. The cop standing by Velma. Remember? I told you that I was at St. Regis. Did you check that out?'

'Yeah, we did check that out,' Wagner said. 'They apologized for not being able to do anything with those ears of yours but said that operation would be beyond their surgical capabilities.'

'Fine,' said Collins, 'but you know I couldn't have killed Kowalski. You know I was at the clinic.'

'Murder for hire is still murder,' Wallace said. 'It makes no difference who pulled the trigger – or wielded the club in this case.' She eyed Tsunami but he didn't react. Albanese got the second cuff on Collins, who now had both hands behind his back.

216

Wagner walked up to Collins and stared into his eyes. 'By the way, dirtball, your little lady there,' he said, pointing to Velma, 'was about ready to abandon your ship, as well. Did you know that?'

Wallace shook her head. Why did Harlen have to stir things up?

'Velma? Nonsense. Tell them, Velma.' Yelland stood silently. 'Is this true sweetheart?' Collins asked. 'Well? Is it?'

Yelland put her cocktail on the floor, then stood up and pulled a pale blue gauze wrap around her. She looked at Wallace as though searching for guidance. Lights. Camera. Action. She needed a script, a director.

'Velma? I'm waiting, girlie. After all I've done for you, were you planning on working for that no-talent scumbag? Are you telling me that you were another one of the rats deserting the ship, Velma?'

'Shut up!' she screamed. 'Shut the fuck up. You're a vile little man. Without me you're nothing, but you treat me like crap.'

'Like crap? Hell, bitch, have another Appletini!' Collins said. He lunged toward her and swung his foot at the cocktail glass by her feet. It hit the edge of the pool, sending shattered pieces of glass flying into the water. 'You're done in Hollywood. Finished. Do you hear me?'

'That's enough!' said Wallace, as Wagner stepped forward to help restrain the furious

Collins, who writhed in Albanese's grasp.

'Stand still,' Wagner said. 'Or I'll bust your fucking arms.'

Keiaho moved forward, but stopped as Wallace pulled up her gun. 'Don't give me any problems, big guy,' she said. 'Been there, done that. You're coming, too.'

The bodyguard held up his hands and stepped away from the fray. Wallace nodded and signaled for him to backup even more. 'Mr. Collins?' he said.

'Do what they say, Keiaho,' Collins said. 'Don't get yourself shot over this. We'll be home within an hour, and the LAPD will be counting the cost for a long time.'

Wagner approached the bodyguard. 'Give me your hands.'

Like a docile bear, Keiaho let Wagner cuff him.

'Stay there,' Wallace said as she walked over to Velma, who was looking both scared and confused as she fumbled for her cigarettes and lit one.

'This is not good,' Velma said. 'I need to speak with my casting agent.'

'Yeah, and I think he would appreciate a call from you, but first, we need some questions answered,' Wallace said.

'What kind of questions?' Velma's eyes locked on Collins.

'You conked Trey Brightman on the head this morning?' Wallace said. Velma started to shake her head. 'Save it, honey. You want to tell us why?'

'You've been seeing Pounder?' spat Collins.

'Shut the fuck up,' said Wagner.

'We can talk here, or at the Precinct,' said Wallace. 'What was the beef with Pounder ... Mr. Brightman.'

Velma nodded toward Collins. 'You won't let him hurt me?'

'You're safe,' said Wallace. 'Mr. Collins – the second – is going to jail.'

'Okay,' said Velma. 'I guess it doesn't make any difference now. The deal's screwed anyway. We had a deal, me and my casting agent, to star in some of Zane Kowalski's new movies.'

'You fucking traitorous bitch!' Collins said.

'I won't tell you again,' said Wagner, easing up Collins' cuffed wrists, making him wince. 'Shut up!'

'Up yours,' Velma said, flipping him the bird.

'That's enough,' Wallace said. 'Go on with why you smacked Brightman on the bean.'

'Like I was saying before he butted in,' she said, gesturing toward the red-faced Collins. 'We had a deal all worked out with Kowalski. We were supposed to meet and sign it tonight. Mr. Orwell, my casting agent said it seemed like poor Zane was barely dead when Brightman called him and said the deal was scrapped but he was willing to negotiate a new one. Mr. Orwell said that Brightman was offering me a two-picture deal and then, based on how those went, we could talk about the future. I knew what he was up to. I heard on the street that Mr. Big Shot Brightman was telling people he wanted to head in a new direction. That he was only signing me for you know, continuity ... is that the right word?'

'Yes,' Albanese said. 'Go on.'

'He wanted continuity – during the transition. But Mr. Orwell said Brightman was signing me to help secure the deal with the distributor and once they inked a contract, he would probably drop me.'

'Brightman wanted to go in a new direction?' Wallace asked. 'What direction would that have been?'

'He wanted to replace me with that slut, Sadie Monaghan.'

'Sadie Monaghan?' Wallace asked. 'So Kowalski's partner wanted Kowalski's old girlfriend to star in his movies. How did they team up?'

'Isn't it obvious? They were conspiring together.'

'Look who's calling the kettle black,' Collins said.

'Shut up,' Velma said. 'Look, Officer, Monaghan was fucking Trey Brightman in order to get the top roles. Why do you think he was going to feature her instead of me?

220

Not based on talent I'll tell you. Not based on looks, either. She was screwing his brains out so he would put her in the best shows. Kowalski told me and Mr. Orwell that he was dropping Monaghan. She was on her way out and I was to be his number one star.'

'What a laugh,' Collins said. 'Do you honestly think he would base his entire future on a worn-out whore like you?'

'I'll show you how worn-out I am,' Velma said, and ran toward the handcuffed man.

'Wait a minute, wait a minute,' Wagner said.

Albanese grabbed Velma.

'Everybody calm down,' Wallace said. 'Okay, Velma, so you're saying Monaghan and Kowalski were going to split?'

'Yes. And I heard it straight from the horse's mouth. Kowalski had been saying for ages that he was going to ditch her. Said she didn't have my ... *presence.* I think you boys should go talk to Miss Monaghan.'

'And Brightman,' Wallace said. 'He wasn't in a position to offer a staring role until Kowalski was out of the way.'

'I told you I didn't kill the bastard,' Collins said. 'Now take these cuffs off. They hurt.'

'Collins, you're under rest for burglary, not murder. Now be quiet,' Wallace said.

'What about me?' said Keiaho.

'Just chill, Tsunami,' said Wagner.

'You know, when Coombs and I were doing

221

the neighborhood Q and A,' Albanese said, 'Diaz and Herdez reported a witness saying a man and woman were arguing big-time. Just after midnight. I didn't think much of it till now. Up on Laurel Canyon, people argue over goddam sprinklers hitting each other's gardens. Maybe the witness heard Monaghan and Kowalski fighting. Maybe he had told her about his plans. The timeframe is right.'

'I'm going to call downtown and tell them we are going after Brightman and Monaghan,' Wallace said. 'They sure as hell look like prime suspects to me. Albanese, if you will take Collins and the man-mountain downtown and process them, we'll meet up with you there.'

'Don't you want me to go with you to get those two?' Albanese asked.

'No. I think Wagner and I can handle it. We'll get some uniforms for backup.'

'What about me, sugar?' Velma asked.

'You're free to go, sweetpea,' said Wagner, 'but we'll need a statement later on. No more hitting people with your shoe. Give your manager a call. He's probably having a nervous breakdown about now.'

Velma gathered up her things and headed inside. She stuck her tongue out at Collins as she passed by.

'Better find a guy who still thinks you're cute, baby,' he sneered, 'because you are done, done, done.'

'Send me a postcard from jail,' she said.

Albanese waited until Velma had disappeared from sight, then he guided Collins into the house. A laugh made Wallace turn. Wagner was slapping Keiaho on the back and the bodyguard said something else that made him laugh harder.

'Do you mind?' she said. 'Get him into the car with Collins.'

At the front door, they waved Albanese off.

'Well, you ready, Phil?' Wagner said.

'I'm going to call in for backup before we leave.'

'You really think we're going to need it?'

'The last time we didn't get uniformed backup was – oh yeah, a few hours ago.'

'It went bad. Besides, a movie producer and a porn star are not exactly a room full of lowlifes. You really think there is going to be trouble?'

'You saw the pictures of what used to be Kowalski's face.'

They walked back into the house to lock up, passing through the sun parlor and into the living room. The click of footprints made Wallace spin and reach for her gun. A bleached blonde with a pneumatic figure swayed toward them.

'Well, I'll be damned,' Wagner said. 'Dawn.'

'Who is Dawn?'

'My fantasy.'

223

The maid came over and looked at the two detectives. 'You're back. Who's your friend?'

'This is Detective Wallace.'

'Hello. I'm Dawn. Where is Mr. Collins? I saw Mr. Keiaho leaving in handcuffs and he said he quit.'

'Mr. Collins is under arrest. Tsunami, too, while we make inquiries. Velma has packed her bags, as well.'

'Mr. Collins is under arrest? Now what do I do?'

'Turn out the lights,' Wagner said. 'The party's over.'

24

Please enter password

Coombs had tried everything she could think of. She thought again and tapped in *'Sadie'*.

Password incorrect. Please type in correct password.

'Any luck?' said Reyes.

'Not yet,' said Coombs. 'Kowalski's hiding something here, but I don't know what. Give me a second.' For the next few minutes, she went through the access protocols in the computer's operating system – a path most normal users wouldn't even be aware of. Finally she found the key – a low-level, question-based security password. A note read: 'If you do not remember your password, enter your email address and we will send you a reminder.'

'Got you,' she muttered under her breath.

'What is it?' said Sal.

'He's locked the door but left the catflap open.'

'What?'

'Nothing,' said Coombs. She clicked for an email reminder and smiled.

Brooks leaned on her cubicle wall. 'Wallace called. Albanese is bringing in Collins. He confessed to being behind the burglary. Wallace said he was going to be cut out of the porn business by Kowalski's deal. As for the killing of Kowalski, she said she thinks they can make a case against Brightman and possibly Monaghan. She and Wagner are going to pick them up.'

'Trey Brightman and Sadie Monaghan?' said Reyes.

'It seems they've been having a relationship behind Kowalski's back,' said Brooks. 'Kowalski was trying to cut Monaghan out of his business, and Trey took exception.'

'Big-time!' said Coombs.'

'Phil was right all along,' said Reyes. 'She said Monaghan was acting, but I couldn't see it.'

'Call it female intuition,' said Brooks. 'I

225

stopped trying to understand women after my second wife walked out.' He gave Coombs a quick glance. 'They're not all bad, though.'

'Gee, thanks, Sarge,' she said.

'Speaking of exes,' said Reyes. 'I gotta get out of here, Ray. It's my kid's birthday.' He looked at his watch, then sighed. 'Damn. When did they call?'

'I don't know. Five minutes maybe. Why? What's wrong?'

'Nando's present. If Albanese is coming in, he could bring it with him.' He pulled out his cell phone and called Wallace.

'Phil? It's Sal. Hey, did you guys already leave the site? Shit. Yeah. Nando's present is in your trunk. No. There's nothing you can do now. I'll wait until you get here. Yeah. Be careful. See ya in a few.'

'Too late, eh? Too bad. Well, why don't you finish your report and then as soon as they get back, you can leave,' Brooks said.

'Okay. There's not a lot of choice in the matter.'

He turned and walked back toward his desk, bracing himself to call Pam and explain the delay.

Coombs opened Kowalski's emails again and the password reminder was there in his inbox. Coombs laughed when she saw it: *ScarletMays.*

'Hey, Sal,' she said. 'I'm in.' She typed the

226

password and hit Return.

Reyes hurried back. 'Great work. Shall we see what Mr. Kowalski has been hiding from us?'

Coombs double-clicked the folder marked index. It opened into two folders labeled 'Stills' and 'Movies'. She opted for the former. There were hundreds of files. 'Oh. Bit of an anticlimax,' she said. 'It's probably just going to be more porn.'

'Why would Kowalski put a password on it, though?' asked Reyes. 'Open one.' He scooted the chair around so he could see better.

Coombs dragged the mouse over a selection of the JPEG thumbnails and opened them. One after the other, the images flicked open. They were all locker-room shots of a cheerleader and a football player having sex. 'Gee, what a shocker.'

'Is there any way we can scan through quickly?' he said.

Coombs switched back to a thumbnail view, displaying all the files in miniature. They were much along the same theme. Cheerleader up against the lockers, cheerleader wearing the football player's helmet while giving a blowjob...

'Wait a minute,' Reyes said. He squinted at the small pictures then pointed at the screen. 'Here, open that one.'

'Recognize someone?'

'That's one of Kowalski's upstairs bedrooms,' Reyes said. 'I'm sure of it. Can you enlarge it?'

'What are you looking for?' Coombs said, enlarging the photo. It showed a girl with pigtails crouched on the bed in her underwear. 'Faces?'

'Yeah, sort of. That one isn't too clear. Open another.'

Coombs enlarged the next photo – it was a guy in shorts on the bed with a girl. 'Do you recognize either of them?'

'No. I was thinking the girl looks pretty damn young. You think she's old enough?'

'She only has to be eighteen.'

'I don't think she's eighteen.'

'That's part of the game. They purposely look for kids who look younger than they are. That way the pornographer stays legal and still satisfies the perverts who dream of doing some ten-year-old.' She searched the JPEGs for a face shot of the girl in the bed. 'Here's one,' she said, and left-clicked her mouse.

A picture of a young, attractive, still-developing girl filled her screen. Her ink-black hair was spread on a silk pillow. She had a look of sublime ecstasy on her face. Her small breasts had all but disappeared in her prone position. With her left hand she reached for her shaved pubic area. With her right, she clutched a doll.

'Pretty sick stuff,' said Coombs.

'How old do you think she is now?'

'It's hard to tell. I've seen better quality pics. She could be eighteen. Everybody doesn't develop at the same age. She could be a late-blooming eighteen-year-old.'

'Or she could be twelve.'

'Yes. She could also be fifteen,' Coombs said.

'Fifteen is underage.'

'I know. I just mean we can't tell. Our guesses are anywhere from twelve to twenty.'

'Let's check another file folder.'

For the next half hour. Coombs and Reyes poured over the files in Kowalski's computer. Most of the pictures and nearly every video stored inside the protected zone of his desktop were taken at Kowalski's house. Reyes noticed that there were different wall decorations in the videos. Sometimes a painting, a mirror or a piece of furniture had been added, making the same bedroom appear different. It didn't take much to change the scene since the audience paid little attention to where the action was taking place. It also explained the closet full of paintings they had found that morning.

'Here's a video shot at a pool,' Coombs said. 'Looks like a skinny-dipping party.' She watched for a minute or two. 'I think there are eight girls.'

'That's Kowalski's back yard and his pool,

no doubt. There's the pool-house.'

'This looks like a high school pool party. Only without clothes. If they were in swim-suits, you wouldn't really pay attention, un-less you were a dirty old man.'

Brooks had quietly slipped back into the cubicle. Coombs looked over her shoulder at him. 'We got past the lock,' she said. 'This video, I think, may be a pool party for some of his stars.'

'We think that some of them may be under eighteen,' Reyes said. 'There are definitely adults involved in some of the videos and pictures, but a few of these girls may be underage.'

'They look like teenagers to me,' Brooks said.

'But are they under eighteen?' Reyes asked. 'At eighteen, they're legal.'

Coombs pulled up a video called *Daddy's Home*. The opening scene was a living room – Kowalski's living room. Three young girls sat around laughing, smoking and dancing. An older balding man with a paunch came in. He was dressed in a suit. The audio sug-gested he was supposed to be the dad of one of the three girls. 'Anyone want to guess what's going to happen?'

'This is sick,' Brooks said.

The video rolled on. Daddy bawled out the trio for drinking. He took one of the girls, his movie daughter, and proceeded to spank her.

The two friends received the same treatment. All three girls were curled up with red asses pointed at the camera. Daddy felt bad, showed his remorse and tried to comfort the girls.

'Aw, crap,' Brooks said.

The girls were soon naked and so was Daddy.

'Okay. I think we've seen enough,' Brooks said. He appeared physically ill. 'We don't need to see every one of these kids being abused. I agree with Reyes. I don't think those girls are legal age.'

'Ray,' said Reyes, 'I know this is ugly but we need to look. The killer could be in these videos. Maybe that's why Collins wanted this computer. He could be in one of the videos or God knows what else. Maybe that's why Fontana didn't give the thing to him. He sure wasn't going to get much money pawning the computer, but if there are pics in here of Collins say, blackmail could be a lucrative side business. Maybe one of the girls is some big shot's daughter. What would Daddy pay to keep something like that from getting out?'

'Ray,' Coombs said. 'Sal and I can handle this. I mean, if you want to go get coffee or something.'

Reyes nodded. 'I could use a cup of coffee from Starbucks. Grande, mild with extra cream.'

'I'll have the same,' Coombs said. 'Ask them for two shots of cinnamon, please.'

Brooks smacked his lips as if trying to find moisture in a dry mouth. 'Maybe that's a good idea,' he said. 'Coffee. Sure. It would probably do me good to get a little air I've been inside all day.' He stepped away from the desk and headed for the door.

'I'm guessing maybe half of these girls that we've seen so far are underage,' Reyes said, 'or there is one hell of a plastic surgeon out there worth his weight in gold.'

'No doctor is that good,' Coombs said. She continued opening files. Some familiar faces popped up now and then – Trey Brightman as Johnny Pounder; Velma Vixen; Sadie Monaghan – but mostly young girls.

Another twenty minutes passed. 'Maybe Brooks is right. Maybe we've seen enough. It doesn't appear we re going to get much out of here.'

'You know what? I could finish this up if you want.'

'No, if you can take it, I can,' Coombs said. 'Let's press on.'

The next two folders featured young women, definitely over twenty-one. Five folders to go. They were all marked with the code 'U12'.

'Shit, Sal, you don't think...'

Reyes swallowed. 'I hope not.'

Coombs opened the first folder and

selected the thirteen JPEGs. The computer displayed them like playing cards a second or two between each. The first was Kowalski himself sitting alone on a bed. A young girl entered the room, in an oversize dressing gown.

'I think I'm gonna be sick,' whispered Reyes.

As the rest of the photos opened, Coombs gasped. 'Oh my God.'

Number thirteen was a shot of the two naked figures.

Reyes was frozen to the spot. 'Oh no. Sweet Jesus, no.'

25

Wagner pulled the car into the parking lot of the Mesa Verde Apartments. Wallace released her death grip on the door handle. 'Jesus, where did you learn to drive?'

'Chicago,' Wagner said. 'Like it?'

She shook her head and looked at the apartments. It was a born-again building. Probably built in the 1930s, but recently got a facelift. Wallace remembered reading that the new owners refurbished it inside and out to attract the upwardly mobile. Good incomes and wanting extras. The building was wireless, no doubt. Your choice of cable or satellite hook-ups. Probably a gym in the basement.

The green area was carefully developed to match the new look, which resembled an old adobe from the original Mesa Verde in Colorado. A good neighborhood. She picked up the radio and called the station.

'Where's our backup? I want to finish this.'

The radio buzzed. 'We're two blocks away.'

'Thanks. What d'you think?' she asked Wagner. 'Did Brightman do this all by himself?'

'What do you mean? Are you asking if he swung the club or was in it alone?'

'Both. He sure looks guilty as hell.'

'Between us,' said Wagner, 'I think Kowalski would have kicked the shit out of Brightman. He may have paid the piper and had somebody take Kowalski out, but I can't believe he whacked him himself.'

'A club to the head or to the nuts is a great equalizer. If Brightman, or anyone for that matter, caught Kowalski off guard, it wouldn't take much to cripple the guy, make him defenseless. One blow to the berries and he'd drop like a prom dress.'

Wagner nodded and looked out of the window. 'Here's the backup.'

The marked unit pulled up beside them. It was a duo called Hastings and Marcell. Wagner opened the driver's window.

'We have a possible murder suspect inside.' Wallace leaned over and handed them Brightman's picture. 'I doubt that he's a runner. However, one of you should cover the back of the building, just in case. The other can cover our back inside. I do not want this guy getting out of here, but I don't want any wild-ass gunplay. We need to take him into custody, unharmed if at all possible. Clear?'

'Understood,' Officer Hastings said. Marcell nodded.

'When we're done here, we have one more to pick up. A female suspect. We'll need you for that one, as well.'

'Lead the way,' Hastings said.

'First, we need to get Mr. Brightman out of apartment two hundred,' Wallace said.

'You take the back,' Hastings said to the other officer. 'Here's the taser. I'll back them up with Tulip.'

'Tulip?' Wallace asked. 'Who the hell is Tulip?'

Hastings presented a shotgun. 'This is her. And don't worry, we haven't lost a perp yet.'

'Uh-huh,' Wallace said. 'Let's remember who the good guys are, okay? We want to take the – er – perp alive.'

'Me and Tulip,' Hastings said. 'We gotcha covered.'

'Let's go,' Wagner said.

The lobby continued the theme of the Mesa Verde with native Colorado columbine as the plant du jour. Wallace identified herself, Wagner and Hastings to the concierge.

'There isn't going to be any shooting or tear gas, is there?' he asked. 'Should I warn the other residents?'

'We don't expect any problems. However, alerting the residents in any adjoining apartment or apartments might be a good idea. Tell them to stay put.'

'There is only one adjoining apartment, two-oh-one. That belongs to the Garfields. Fortunately they are on vacation in Mozambique.'

'Well, then the Garfields should be just fine,' Wagner said. 'Come on, Phil, this joker Brightman isn't going to put up a fight.'

Wallace took hold of Wagner's arm and pulled him toward a potted tree in the foyer.

'You don't get it, do you, Harlen?' she whispered. 'There wasn't supposed to be a problem at the Mexican Smuggler, either, but that didn't work out so well, did it? Man, you'll be lucky if Siley doesn't have your ass in a sling by breakfast.'

'This is like the nineteenth time somebody brought that shit up today. Okay. I get it. I blew the call. Why the hell does it bother you so damned much?'

'Because you lied to me,' Wallace said. 'You told me you had cleared that whole deal, but Brooks never said okay. Captain Siley never even heard about it until he got

236

the call that Kahn had been shot.'

Wagner looked down at his feet. 'I know, and I'm gonna have to live with it. Can we worry about the man upstairs first?'

'Sure,' said Wallace. 'But when you start looking out for me, I'll return the favor. Come on.'

'Officers?' the concierge said. 'Excuse me. I don't know if this makes a difference, but Mr. Brightman has a guest. A female. I thought you should know – in case he decides to take her hostage or something.'

'Do you know the name of his guest?' Wallace asked.

'Excuse me?' the concierge said. He gave a look of disgust. 'I know everything that goes on in this building. It is a Miss Sadie Monaghan. A fairly frequent visitor of late.'

'Well, that's going to work out well,' Wallace said. 'Now, if you could give us a little more help. We have the right to enter that apartment. We can break the door down or we can open it with a key.'

'Here,' the concierge said. He reached into a small cabinet and removed a single key. He handed it to Wallace. 'That's a passkey. Now, please, try not to smash the place up. I like my job.'

'We'll do our best,' Wallace said. She headed for the elevator, favoring her swollen ankle. 'Hastings – tell your partner that we have both of the suspects in one place.' She pushed the up button and the door to the elevator opened. Without another word, she stepped inside. Wagner, Hastings and Tulip followed. Hastings made the call to his partner.

When the doors opened again, the trio stepped into the second-floor hallway. 'Stay back about ten feet,' Wallace said to Hastings. 'Don't shoot unless they start firing. Understand?'

'Me and Tulip will hold until we see the whites of their eyes.'

Wallace took a deep breath. 'You know what?' she said. 'Change of plan. You stay in the hall. If either Brightman or Monaghan gets past us, then you take them.' Wallace stopped and looked at Hastings. 'Alive. But you knew that right? We want both of them alive.'

Hastings smiled. 'Gotcha covered.'

'So much for backup, eh, Phil?' Wagner said. 'Sometimes you just gotta do whatcha gotta do. That's the way this job is.'

'Unlock the door quietly,' Wallace said. 'Then knock and go.'

Wagner inserted the master key and slowly turned it in the lock. The bolt clicked. Then he grasped the knob and banged on the door with the butt of his gun. 'Police. Open the door.' He banged again. 'Police.' He turned the handle and stepped in, gun leveled. 'Clear.'

Wallace entered the apartment behind him. They were in a hallway. One door on the left, two on the right. 'Police,' she said loud enough for anyone in the apartment to hear. No response.

Wagner pushed open the first door. 'Bathroom's clear.' A scream came from the door opposite. Wagner took a step back and launched a foot toward the handle. Wallace was there, covering him.

The handle splintered open to reveal Trey Brightman. He stood in front of the bed, his underwear halfway to decency, his hands up.

'What the fuck...'

'Hold it,' said Wallace, pointing her gun at his chest.

Monaghan sat naked in the bed, the covers pulled up to her chin.

'Pull 'em up,' Wagner said. 'We don't want to see that.'

Brightman tugged up his briefs. 'What in the hell is going on?'

'You're both under arrest for the murder of Zane Kowalski,' Wallace said. 'Let's get dressed.'

'Murder? You've got to be kidding,' Brightman said.

'Less talk, more getting dressed,' Wagner said.

'Would one of you hand me my robe?' Monaghan said.

'Modesty fails you,' Wallace said.

Wagner grabbed a pink silk robe with a white faux-fur collar and cuffs. 'Here,' he said. 'At least these collar and cuffs match.'

'You're so funny I forgot to laugh,' Monaghan said. She slipped the robe on as she slid from the bed. 'You're making a mistake. We didn't have anything to do with killing Zane.'

'She's telling you the truth, officer,' Brightman said.

'Take him to the living room,' Wallace said. 'I'll stay with Miss Monaghan while she dresses. Read him his rights.'

'Grab your shit and let's go,' Wagner said.

Brightman picked up his clothes that had been thrown over the back of a chair and headed down the hall.

Wallace stepped over to the bedroom door and closed it. 'Stop me if you've heard this one. You have the right to remain silent. Anything you say can and will be used against you in a court of law. You have the right to have an attorney present during questioning. If you cannot afford an attorney, one will be appointed for you. Do you understand these rights?'

'Yes,' Monaghan said. 'But you can't seriously think that we had anything to do with Zane's death.'

'Do you wish to make a statement?'

'Do you mind turning around – I need to

240

get dressed?'

'You're kidding me, right? In your line of work?'

'I'm not at work.'

'Put your clothes on, honey.'

Monaghan let the robe slip to the floor and pulled a pair of black panties from the dresser. She slipped them on and reached for the matching brassiere. 'Why do you think we're involved with his murder anyway?' She fastened her bra and closed the drawer.

'You said you dropped him off somewhere around midnight, give or take. Then you said that you went home without anything further happening between you two. Witnesses put a woman and man outside arguing around twelve-fifteen. That was you and Kowalski. The medical examiner said that Kowalski was killed between midnight and 2:00 a.m. Do you want me to go on?'

Monaghan opened the closet and removed a pair of jeans from the wire shelf.

'Why not?' she said with a sly smile. 'You seem to think that you have it all figured out.'

Wallace kept her gun drawn and watched Monaghan squeeze in the jeans.

'You argued. Kowalski was going to drop you, wasn't he? He'd lined up a more lucrative replacement preferred by the suits at CatwalkG – Velma Vixen.'

Sadie snorted and picked up a baby blue T-

241

shirt from the floor, pulling it over her head. 'Whatever. I'm telling you Velma Vixen is over the hill. If it weren't for plastic surgery, she'd look like Jabba the Slut.'

Her demeanor was strangely confident. Wallace remembered back a few hours when a weeping Monaghan had put on a performance worthy of an Oscar. *This is just another act,* she reminded herself.

'Kowalski thought he had considered everything, but he didn't figure on one thing: you and Trey doing the nasty behind his back. You tried to reason with him, argued with him, and when that didn't work, you and Trey killed him. Everyone wins, except Kowalski, of course.'

A frown creased Monaghan's brow. 'What do you mean, *behind his back?*'

Wallace was momentarily taken aback. 'You and Brightman weren't playing checkers in here just now. You were cheating on Kowalski with his partner.'

'Cheating on him?' She laughed. 'Are you for real?'

'Sure I am. You two were hot and heavy. An item.'

Monaghan put her hands on her hips, turned her head slightly so that she was looking at the ceiling and assumed a huffy pose. Then she looked at Wallace with a curious stare and said, 'You're serious, right? Unbelievable. Okay, let me explain it to you. At first me and Kowalski were an item but that was years ago and private. Not anymore. He took me to parties. He took publicity photos with me on his arm or lying by the pool. That's it. There was no more to the relationship than a photo op.'

'I don't follow,' Wallace said.

'Women didn't turn him on, okay? He couldn't get it up with me.'

'You're saying Zane Kowalski was homo-sexual?'

'Hey, Phil,' shouted Wagner from the other room, 'I got Sal on the line. Says it's urgent.'

Monaghan shook her head. 'I didn't say he was gay.' She had a painfully sad look on her face. The mask had slipped. 'Don't you get it? That's not what I meant at all.'

26

'I don't really want to be here,' Brooks said. 'You should have taken Coombs.'

Reyes parked the car outside of the Cortez' bungalow on Silver Lake Boulevard, an almost exact replica of every other house on the street. Three rooms probably, and all no doubt occupied by large, low-income Latino families.

'Yeah, I know how you feel,' said Reyes.

243

'I'd rather not be here, either. I'd rather be playing with my seven-year-old son who I haven't seen for eight days.' He checked the rearview mirror to see if the agents from Child Protection Services were behind him. He was still feeling bruised from the grilling Pam had given him when he'd called to say he would be late. Her closing words, the quietest she uttered in the whole conversation, bounced around behind his eyes, giving him a headache: *It's always the same, Salvador. It always was.* The worst thing about it was she had a point. He unlocked his seat belt. 'Ray, you know that if Coombs left the station, FID would have busted her ass. They would have also nailed you for authorizing it and probably me for helping her disobey the order.'

'I know. I know all that. I...'

'Look, the two CPS agents will do most of the work with Mrs. Cortez – mostly in Spanish, I guess. We'll just talk to the husband.'

'Hey, I said I know. That shit just hit me kind of hard today.'

'Let's do it.'

Reyes took a deep breath, switched off the engine and stepped from the car. Brooks climbed heavily out of his seat. Reyes waved to the two agents. They were both dressed smart but casual. *They look like they've done this a hundred times.*

'Let me do the intros,' said Reyes. 'Mrs.

Cortez knows me.'

Together they walked to the front door and Reyes knocked. Inside, he heard the chatter of a woman's voice, and the tapping of heels on a wooden floor. Mrs. Cortez opened the door wiping her hand on a dishtowel. Panic instantly filled her eyes.

'Oh,' she said. 'Is something wrong?'

Reyes introduced Brooks and the two CPS agents, Donna Wells and Felix Baumgardner in Spanish. Both gave broad smiles. 'We'd like to come in and talk with you,' he said. 'It's important.'

Reluctantly Mrs. Cortez backed away from the entrance. 'I'm in the middle of cooking dinner.'

Reyes translated for Brooks, before switching back to Manuela's tongue. 'Is your husband home?'

'No. He's at work.'

'That's fine. What time did he go in?'

'Six o'clock.' She looked down at the floor. 'It's a long shift. He says they have two boats to finish. Will you tell me what's the matter? Is Miguel in some sort of trouble? Maybe I should call him.'

'Perhaps we could come in,' said Reyes.

Manuela looked back into the hall nervously, then signaled for them to follow her.

The group walked behind Manuela toward the kitchen, where the spicy aroma of Mexican cooking made Reyes' stomach grumble.

He realized he'd eaten only almonds all day. Brooks grabbed Reyes' arm, and mouthed 'the husband'. Reyes nodded and pulled free, then mouthed back, 'not yet'.

'Mmm. Smells good,' Reyes said.

'It's chicken with rice,' she said, allowing herself a small smile.

'Mrs. Cortez,' Reyes said, 'when you cleaned Mr. Kowalski's house, did you ever have the need to leave your daughter there, alone?'

There was obvious hesitation. Reyes knew that there must be a thousand thoughts running through her head and all of them were bad.

'*Si.*' she nodded. 'Sometimes.' She choked out the words in short staccato English. 'Mr. Kowalski. He love Sara. If she asleep. Or maybe she is playing. Then I finish my work so it is – time to go. He say...' Her eyes dropped as she searched for the right phrase.

'You can speak Spanish,' said Reyes gently.

Manuela didn't seem to hear and gestured with her hand twirling it as if signaling the word to come. 'He would sometimes say to – let her be. You know? I could leave her. I get her when I go home. It was good for me. Sara, too. She played.' Mrs. Cortez opened a package of tortilla shells. 'I don't understand. Please, tell me. What has happened? Why are they here?' she asked, pointing to the CPS agents.

'Mrs. Cortez, I'm sorry. There is no easy way to say this. We have good reason to suspect that Mr. Kowalski was sexually abusing Sara.'

'Uhh...' Manuela Cortez exhaled as though she had been hit in the stomach. The package of tortilla shells dangled loosely in her hand as she made the sign of the cross then reached for a kitchen chair. Agent Wells took her shoulders and guided her into the seat. 'No,' she said, still gasping for air, then in Spanish again– 'Not my Sara. No, no, Santa Maria help me.'

'Mrs. Cortez,' said Wells, 'my name is Donna. We need to speak with Sara. Is she home?'

Tears were filling her eyes as she nodded. 'Sara,' she said. 'Sara? Come here.'

Brooks shifted on the spot and Manuela held a hand to her temple. Sara came into the kitchen. 'Yes, Mama?' The moment she saw the gathering of adults and her mother's worried face, she hurried to her mother's arms and hung on tightly.

'Mrs. Cortez, it might be easier for everyone if you were to ask Sara.'

She looked up and shook her head. 'I can't.'

'What is it, Mama?' asked Sara.

'Do you want me to do it?' Agent Wells asked.

Reyes looked at her, then back to Mrs. Cortez. He could sense Brooks in his peripheral vision, head bowed. He didn't need to understand the Spanish to understand the awful tension looming in the kitchen. Manuela suddenly grasped Sara's face with both hands and held her firm, looking into her daughter's eyes. Sara started to cry.

'Sara, tell me, did Señor Kowalski ever touch you?' Sara shook and her lips trembled. For a moment it looked as though she was trying to pull away, but Manuela was holding her tightly. 'Sara?'

The little girl gave a few quick nods, and grabbed her mother's wrists with both hands. Mrs. Cortez pulled her daughter close and hugged her even tighter.

The CPS agents both looked at Reyes, who was feeling like shit. He waited until Sara lifted her face from her mother's shoulder.

'Sara?' said Reyes. 'Do you remember me? I was at Mr. Kowalski's house this morning. Then you colored some pictures at my office. Do you remember me?'

'Yes,' she said, her voice trembling.

'Sara, this is Miss Wells. She wants to ask you a few questions. She's a nice lady. Can you answer a few questions for her?'

Sara looked at her mother.

She nodded, as though unable to speak.

'Okay,' Sara said.

Wells squatted in front of Sara and, as gently as she could, asked the questions

Reyes knew he never could. Sara was brave, and soon the tears had stopped. Reyes couldn't help but get angry and think of Nando when Sara talked about what Kowalski had done, all paid for with bribes of sweets and dolls. Sometimes he hurt her when he touched her 'down there'.

'My baby, my precious little baby,' Mrs. Cortez said in Spanish. 'Why didn't you tell me?'

Sara sobbed. 'Mr. Kowalski told me not to tell you.'

Her mother took Sara's hand. 'You should have told me, baby.'

'But Mr. Kowalski said not to,' she said, her body shaking with sobs. 'I told Daddy, though.'

Reyes turned to give Brooks a knowing look, then spoke in Spanish once more. 'Mrs. Cortez, you said your husband is at work right now?'

'Yes,' she said. 'He just left before you got here. Maybe ten minutes. You know? Before you came.'

'And this place he works, what was the name of it again?'

'Jonathan Laird Boat Works.'

Reyes translated for the others. 'Thank you.'

Mrs. Cortez shook her head. 'No bothering Miguel, please.'

'We need to talk with him,' Reyes said, trying to avoid explaining the obvious to a woman already in pain.

Mrs. Cortez ran her hand through her daughter's black hair She was still frightened and now even more confused. 'I don't understand,' she said, then came the dawn. The look on her face went from sadness to horror. 'Oh no. No, *señor.* You are wrong. He is a sweet man. He wouldn't hurt Mr. Kowalski.'

'Mama, Mama...' Sara said.

'Shh,' Mrs. Cortez said. 'Hush, little one.'

'What did she say?' Brooks asked.

'She said her husband is a nice guy and couldn't have hurt Kowalski,' Reyes said. 'Mrs. Cortez. What kind and what color of vehicle does your husband drive?'

'A tan Ford truck. But he's painting it.'

'Is it part gray?'

'Yes.'

'What?' Brooks asked.

'He's fixing the truck up. It's tan but it is primed. Gray primer.' Reyes turned to Mrs. Cortez. 'Okay. We have to go. These two agents will stay with you until we have a chance to talk to your husband.'

Reyes signaled Baumgardner to follow him into the living room. 'Stay with her until we call you,' he said. 'And don't let her use the phone. I'd like to make this as easy as we can regarding her husband. I don't really want to be chasing him down the oh-five.'

'I understand,' Baumgardner said.

Brooks was standing at the door with his hands on his hips. 'Sal, you ready?'

'Yeah, I'm ready.'

Reyes and Brooks said goodbye to Sara and Mrs. Cortez. As a parent, it felt awful to leave a mother and her daughter in tears, but as a cop he was glad to be going. Let the professionals deal with it.

'Well, that sucked,' Brooks said, as he fastened his seat belt.

'It's going to suck some more.' Reyes called the station. 'Coombs?'

'Go ahead,' Coombs said. 'What happened?'

'Unfortunately, there is a very strong possibility that Mr. Cortez may be our killer.'

'Oh, man,' Coombs said. 'What are you doing?'

'We have to go to the Jonathan Laird Boat Works. Miguel Cortez is supposed to be at work there.'

'I'll pull up the address.' A few seconds later she gave them the location off Sepulveda. 'You guys be careful.'

'Yeah. We'll let you know when we have him in custody. You might want to have the patrol for that area standing by in the parking lot in case he bolts. Have them locate and block in a Ford pickup that is partially tan but mostly gray primer.'

'Will do.'

251

Reyes disconnected. 'Here we go.'

'If Mr. Cortez did kill Kowalski, then he's going to jail,' Brooks said. 'If he ever gets out, he'll be deported.'

'You're probably right.'

'Yeah, and you know what?'

'What?'

'It sucks.'

27

Reyes took the ramp off the highway and followed the sign to the Jonathan Laird Boat Works. Miguel Cortez' truck was parked in the lot, and behind it was the marked unit. Two cops called Williams and Anderson leaned against the trunk of their squad car. They stood up straighter as Reyes parked beside them.

'Okay. Here's the deal,' Reyes said without preliminaries. 'The suspect's gonna be scared shitless. He's an illegal and he's wanted for questioning in a murder. Williams, you take the back by the loading dock. Anderson, stay by his truck. My gut says that he will make a run for it. Don't use deadly force unless you're threatened. I hate to say it, but he's not a bad guy.'

The two uniforms took up their positions.

Reyes and Brooks entered the Boat Works through a metal front door. The floor was painted concrete. The walls were covered with paneling and photographs of boats and ships. There was a section for boats built by the Laird company, all with a distinctive 'JL' crest.

'Looks like they've put quite a few on the high seas,' Brooks said.

A small, cheap coffee table covered with magazines and newspapers sat in between a dark blue sofa and two chairs. In the far corner of the room was a gray metal desk. Behind it sat a balding uniformed security guard.

'Can I help you?' he asked. He stood up, placed his cap on his head, hooked his thumbs under his Sam Brown belt and stood like a John Wayne marine. He was armed and overconfident: a dangerous combination.

'How you doing? I'm Detective Reyes, this is Detective Brooks. We're with Hollywood Precinct. And you are?'

'Lionel Jones,' he said, tapping a cockeyed badge. 'I'm in charge of the Night Security Division of the Jonathan Laird Boat Works.'

'We might be able to use a little help,' Brooks said. 'How many guards do you have on duty tonight?'

'Oh, well, there's just me. But Ferris pitches in from time to time.'

'Who is Ferris?' Brooks asked.

'He's the maintenance guy but he'll do almost anything you ask.'

'That's okay,' Reyes said. 'Could we see the foreman or manager?'

'Sure.' Jones made a phone call. In a few minutes a middle-aged man with sandy hair and glasses came into the lobby and introduced himself as Jimbo Peters, the foreman. He wore a white short-sleeved shirt, a red tie and a pocket protector filled with pens.

Reyes identified himself and Brooks once more, then came to the point. 'We need to speak with one of your employees. Miguel Cortez. Is there a chance you can ask him to come out here and talk with us?'

'Miguel?' Peters asked. 'I hope he isn't in trouble – he's one of the best craftsmen we've got.'

'I understand,' Reyes said. 'Maybe you could answer a question or two about Mr. Cortez for us first.'

'I'm not sure I should do that. Isn't there some kind of confidentiality thing involved here?'

'Oh, sorry,' Reyes said. 'I didn't know you were a lawyer.'

'I'm not a lawyer.'

'Doctor?'

'No.'

'Priest?'

'Okay, okay. I get it. I was just trying to

protect my employees,' Peters said. 'Miguel is really talented. I'd hate to lose him.'

'Why do you think you'd lose him? I said I only wanted to talk to him.'

'Look, I don't want any trouble.'

'Miguel is also an undocumented alien. No green card. Is that the problem, Mr. Peters?'

He nodded. 'Isn't that what this is about?'

'How about if we ask the questions? Cortez' shift is 6:00 p.m. to 6:00 a.m. Is that correct?'

'Until we get this order for the Saudis out of here, yes. Lots of overtime.'

'Can you tell me if Cortez was here for his entire shift yesterday?'

Peters pressed his lips together. 'No.'

'No you can't tell me, or no he wasn't here for his entire shift?'

'He wasn't here for any of it. He got one of the guys from days to cover.'

'Maybe you should ask him to step out here. It might be easier and safer for everybody. I wouldn't mention to him that we're cops.'

'I don't like the sound of this,' Peters said. 'Is there going to be trouble? I have a lot of employees in there.'

'We'll try to do things as peacefully as possible. Could you go get Mr. Cortez, please?'

Peters entered the factory area through swinging double doors marked with a red and white sign: 'Employees Only'. The sound of sawing buzzed through before the doors closed again.

Reyes turned to Jones. 'When Cortez joins us, could you move toward those doors,' he said, pointing to the factory entrance, 'and block his way, in case he decides to run.'

Jones' eyes widened and he nodded. 'Sure.'

'Try to not let him notice what you're up to. We don't want him getting any more nervous than he probably will be. And I see you're armed. Under no circumstances draw your gun.'

Jones' face fell for a second. 'Whatever you say, Detective.'

'Ray, take the front entrance to the building in case he gets by me and heads for the parking lot.'

Reyes moved to the sitting area. That would direct the talk away from both sets of doors and allow Brooks and Jones to react should they need to.

Peters returned a few minutes later with Miguel Cortez. He wore a white hard hat and a grubby gray T-shirt covered in sawdust. He looked calm enough as his eyes took in Brooks and Reyes.

'Do you speak English. Mr. Cortez?' Reyes asked.

'Yes. Not well, maybe.'

Reyes identified himself and his partner Brooks as police officers. He thought he saw

Cortez' Adam's apple bob. He pulled off his work gloves nervously. *We'll start there.*

'Are those new gloves, Mr. Cortez?'

Cortez looked at his hands, then shrugged. 'Yes. I need to change gloves because they get sticky from the stains and sealers.'

'All of the guys replace their gloves frequently,' Peters said. 'They're provided by the company.'

'That's great, Mr. Peters. Please let Mr. Cortez answer my questions.'

'Sure. I was only trying to help!' he said under his breath.

'Could you tell me where your old gloves are?' said Reyes.

Cortez shook his head. 'Thrown away.'

'Would you mind giving us a sample of your hair for a DNA test?'

Cortez shrugged.

'Where were you last night about midnight?'

'Here. At work.' Cortez glanced at his boss, who dropped his chin in a silent sigh. Reyes was stepping forward to make the arrest, when Cortez grabbed Peters' arm and hurled his boss toward Reyes. The two men fell backward over the small coffee table.

As Reyes pushed Peters off him he saw Cortez smash into Jones, driving him backward through the doors and into the factory.

Reyes jumped up. 'Tell the guys outside!' he shouted to Brooks.

'Don't damage my yachts!' he heard Peters yell as he ran through the double doors. Jones was sprawled on the floor, already unclipping his firearm.

'Don't you fucking dare!' shouted Reyes as he set off after Cortez.

The suspect was racing toward the back of the factory between two massive yachts. Scattered around were machine parts and racks of equipment. Reyes counted six visible employees. They all stopped their work and turned toward Reyes.

'Stop Miguel!' Reyes yelled. A large Hispanic man, holding a plane, moved into his path. *A friend of Cortez?* 'Police! Get back. Get back.'

The man glanced at the fleeing Cortez, then at Reyes. Reyes waved him out of the way and sprinted past.

Cortez hit the wide rust-colored doors at the back of the plant. Reyes grabbed his radio. 'Cortez is exiting the building. At the back. Loading dock. Head him off.'

He entered a dark freight staging area. Did Cortez go outside or was he hiding among the boxes and stacks of wood? Reyes drew his gun.

The crates formed wooden valleys eight to ten feet high. He moved cautiously looking up and down for Cortez. He peeked around the corner – left, then right. No one was there. The area was lit by a dozen single-bulb overhead lights, which did little to eliminate the gloom.

Reyes twitched as his radio blared. 'This is Williams. The son-of-a-bitch is out here. I'm down. I need help.'

'Shit.' Reyes saw the door swinging and rushed onto the back loading dock.

'Over here.'

Williams was lying on the ground at the base of a concrete platform. Reyes jumped down. 'What the hell happened?'

'He came roaring through the doors and caught me full force. I think I broke my fucking leg.'

Reyes spoke into his radio. 'This is Reyes. Ten-five. Officer down with possible broken leg.'

'Dispatching ambulance. Give me your location.'

'Tell the crew to proceed to the rear of the Jonathan Laird Boat Works on Sepulveda. Officer is in the back by the loading dock.'

'Roger.'

'We also have a suspect still at large. Proceed with caution.'

'Sorry,' Williams said.

The radio broke in. 'This is Anderson. Perp is in the corner of the parking lot where the two fences meet.'

'I'm coming,' Reyes said. 'Where's Brooks?'

'I'm with his truck,' Brooks said.

'Roger. Anderson, stay between Cortez

and the street.'

'Copy.'

Outside, Reyes spotted Cortez as he leaped onto the fence and began crawling up.

'Stop running, Miguel!' Reyes shouted. 'There's nowhere to go.'

Cortez didn't slow. He reached the top, carefully maneuvered over the strands of barbed wire and jumped to the other side.

Anderson reached the corner seconds before Reyes did. Cortez lay crumpled on the ground. Reyes swore at him through the fence. The man was breathing heavily, his face creased with desperation.

'Mr. Cortez, why don't you climb back over and let's talk.' If he didn't convince him to surrender right here, right now, this might end in a bad way. 'I know how you must feel. I have a little kid myself. I'm not sure what I would do if someone did anything to him, but I do know you can't run away from this. Think of Manuela and Sara, man. Just come back over the fence. You won't be hurt.'

Cortez hesitated on the ground. Perhaps he was considering it. Anderson reached for his belt and pulled out his taser. As soon as he saw it, Cortez stood and raced across an empty lot toward the freeway.

'Goddammit,' Reyes said, and threw himself onto the fence. He picked his way over the barbed wire and landed on the other side. Cortez scrambled up the incline toward the San Diego freeway.

Anderson hit the ground beside him.

'Sorry, man – I thought I could take him.'

Reyes didn't bother answering.

Cortez reached the top of the slope, looked back at the officers, then started running alongside of the freeway.

'Suspect is running north along the four-oh-five,' Reyes called over the radio. 'He's on the west shoulder. We are on foot and in pursuit. Any units in the vicinity that can lend a hand, we'd appreciate it.' He could hear cars honking their horns, and the squeal of tires.

'Aw, hell,' Reyes said. At the top of the slope, he saw that Cortez had made it to the center median. 'Anderson, head north along the shoulder, then cross over if you can get ahead of him. I'll stay in close pursuit. Let's try to cut off his escape.'

Reyes waited for the first gap in the traffic and bolted across to the median. Cortez saw him coming and climbed over the concrete barrier separating the northbound and southbound lanes. He sprinted down the center divider.

'Stop, Cortez. Stop, dammit!' The cars and trucks whipped up blasts of air, peppering his face with sand and dust. Without warning, Cortez turned and ran across the traffic lanes toward the far side. Reyes checked traffic, found a small gap and crossed the first lane.

Cortez stumbled, staggered forward and fell into the path of oncoming traffic. Reyes didn't think, he just ran. Cortez was half up as the detective applied a solid tackle, sending both of them onto the trash-covered side shoulder. Reyes heard the crunch of something under his arm.

Cars and trucks hurtled by. The long notes of passing trucks' air horns screamed at the men as they lay still. Cortez placed both palms on the hot pavement to push himself up but Reyes summoned up enough energy to grab the man's right wrist and pull his arm behind his back.

Reyes climbed on Cortez' back, pulled the other arm in and handcuffed him. His elbow was killing him and he could feel blood trickling down his face. 'Are you okay?' he asked Cortez.

'I'm hurt – I think my nose is broken.'

'Yeah, well, we're both hurting, I think. Let me see it.' He stood and pulled the man to his knees, then to his feet. A red gash, bleeding freely, marked the bridge of his nose, but it wasn't misshapen.

'I don't think it's broken. You shouldn't have run, Miguel. I'm arresting you for the murder of Zane Kowalski...'

Cortez didn't seem to be listening as Reyes read him his rights.

Afterward Reyes called on the radio. 'Any units responding to the four-oh-five chase please identify. We're Code Four but I've got a Ten-Eight and would appreciate a ride.'

'Bravo Nine-twelve. We'll be on you in a minute and can give you and your passenger a ride back to your station.'

'Thanks, Bravo Nine-twelve. We'll be the two messed-up guys on the side of the road. One of us is in cuffs.'

'Roger.' He signed off with a laugh. They waited by the side of the road in silence, while Reyes caught his breath.

'Can I have a cigarette?' Cortez asked.

'I don't smoke.'

'I have some. There's a lighter in my pocket.'

Reyes lit a cigarette for him and placed it in his mouth. 'Got it?'

'You said your name was Reyes?'

'Yeah. Salvador Reyes.'

'Can I ask you a question, Salvador?'

'Sure, go ahead. You've got about thirty seconds. There's our ride.'

'You're a Mexican, aren't you?'

'I was born there, yes.'

'Why are you hunting your own kind? We're all Mexicans. We're just like you. We're trying to make a life for our families. You should be helping your own kind.'

The squad car pulled up. Reyes opened the door.

'My own kind, as you call them, don't go around killing people.' He pulled the cigarette from Cortez' mouth, dropped it and crushed the butt. He looked into the man's sad brown eyes and saw they were just like Sara's.

'I'm really sorry this has turned out so very bad for you and your family, but you can't go around killing people because you decide they need to be killed.'

'I did not decide that. Mr. Kowalski decided that.'

Reyes slammed the door.

28

'I'm ready,' Reyes said as he came out of the break-room. His sleeve was pulled up and his arm bandaged where he'd fallen on a broken bottle by the side of the freeway.

'Okay,' Wallace said, 'but you're sure you want me to take the lead on this one? I think Cortez will feel more comfortable telling you what happened.'

'I'd appreciate it if you could take the lead.'

'No problem.'

They headed for interrogation room two. Reyes carried two cups of coffee. He put one in front of Cortez and took a seat opposite him. Wallace checked the video was working, then sat at the head of the table. Reyes Mirandized Cortez formally in English and Spanish. 'Do you understand your rights. Mr. Cortez?'

'Yes.' He took a sip of coffee.

Wallace understood why Reyes felt sorry for the man. He looked broken.

'Why don't you start at the beginning, Mr. Cortez?' Wallace said. 'When and how exactly did you find out about Kowalski and your daughter?'

'Kowalski *es un chi-chi cabrón.*'

'In English, please.'

His face set hard. 'Kowalski – he's a bastard.'

'Please. Just tell us what happened.'

'I got home yesterday, and Manuela was out buying groceries. My darling, my precious daughter Sara was lying on her bed crying. I thought maybe she was upset that she didn't get to go along. But when I asked her what was wrong, she said she didn't want to go with her mama on her cleaning rounds anymore.'

'So this was yesterday?' Wallace asked.

'Yes. That monster called and asked Manuela to start cleaning again the next morning.'

'But Sara didn't say anything to her mommy.'

'No. Kowalski told her not to – he said he'd hurt her mama if she did.'

'Okay. So Sara said she didn't want to go to Kowalski's the next day. Then what did you do?'

'Sara had always seemed to enjoy going along before, so I asked why she didn't want to go. She said she didn't like the games Kowalski played with her. I asked her why not? She said because it hurt when he touched her "down there". *Entiendo?* I was destroyed. I was angry. I didn't know what to do.'

'You should have called the police,' Reyes said.

'Yes, maybe, if I had a green card...' He cut his response short.

Wallace nodded. 'Keep going.'

'I didn't tell Sara's mother. It would have upset her a lot. I told Sara I would take care of things. I took a key to Kowalski's house from my wife's keyring.'

'You took her key? How did your wife get in the next morning?'

Cortez looked at her. 'My wife told me that Kowalski's house was having a security system installed. The front-door key had an alarm activator button on it, like a car key does. The side-doorkey didn't. I figured she wouldn't even notice that one was missing from the ring because she told me she always uses the front door.'

'So you drove over to Kowalski's house instead of going to work?'

'Not right away. I drove around for a while. I didn't know what to do. Then I decided I had to confront him.'

'What time was that?'

'I don't know, but I didn't want to go unarmed. I wanted to scare him. So I went to the Boat Works and took one of the damaged teak dowels from the discard pile. It was the only weapon I could think of.' He took a sip of coffee. 'I drove over to Kowalski's. Several times. I would go there and drive by. I would come back and park, then drive away. I did that for about half an hour. Finally, I parked down the street so my truck wasn't right in front of his house. It was dark inside. I let myself in the side door. No one was home.'

'Let me make sure, for the record, what time it was.'

Cortez thought for a moment. 'It must have been around eleven-thirty, maybe midnight.'

'Okay, go ahead,' Wallace said. 'How soon before Kowalski came in?'

'Not long. I heard noise and hid. A man and a woman came inside. They were arguing. Very loud and very angry.'

'Did you recognize the two people?' Wallace asked.

'No. I'd never seen Kowalski before and I didn't know the woman, either, but she was really mad. She reached out and slapped the guy. That's when he got really angry and told her to...' Cortez stopped and turned toward Reyes.

'What's the matter?' Reyes asked.

Cortez gestured toward Wallace. 'Kowalski said, you know, *profanidad.*'

'That's alright. Please try to use his exact words. Officer Wallace will not be offended by his language.'

Wallace smiled and nodded. *'Gracias.'*

Cortez nodded. 'He said to "get the fuck out of his house, that she was finished in the business". Then he called her a "filthy slut".'

'Did they call each other by their names?'

'I don't think so.'

'Okay. Go on,' Wallace said. 'So the woman left?'

'Yes. Then he made a drink and went upstairs. I saw him go into his bedroom.'

'Where were you?'

'I was downstairs. I don't remember everything that happened but I know I went upstairs. He was standing in front of the TV in his underwear. He turned suddenly. I must have surprised him but he just stood there.'

'Did he know who you were?'

'I don't think at first. Then, there was this look on his face. I can't describe it. Fear? *Arrogancia?* Whatever it was, at the last moment he must have realized what he was watching and tried to turn it off before I saw

268

it. He was too slow. I heard my daughter's voice and rushed in. It was a video of him and my Sara.'

'So that's when you attacked him?' Wallace said.

'I pushed him. I told him who I was. I told him I was going to go to the police. He was drunk and mean and a cocky *hijo de puta*. He laughed at me. No one would believe me, he said. He said that he would claim that I attacked him. We would all be deported, including my little daughter.'

'And what did you do?' Wallace asked, already knowing the unfortunate answer.

'I just stood there. He kept laughing at me. Then he hit the eject button and removed the DVD. He said he would watch it later but he was sure it would be a best-seller.' Reyes drew a deep breath. 'I was no longer thinking. I swung my club and hit his hand. He screamed and dropped the DVD. I bent to pick it up. When I did, he pushed me down and ran from the bedroom. I chased him toward the kitchen. I took a wild swing and caught him in the knee with my club. He went down, falling into the kitchen. I stood over him, and hit him and hit him.' Cortez started to cry. 'I just...'

'Alright, Mr. Cortez,' said Wallace.

'I'll fetch Jaworski,' said Reyes. Wallace nodded and he left the room.

'I'm going to jail,' Cortez sobbed. 'What

will happen to Sara and Manuela?'

'The first thing you need to do is ask for a public defender,' Wallace said. 'I'm not a lawyer, but there may be what they call "extenuating circumstances."'

Reyes and Officer Jaworski entered the room. After Cortez signed his statement, Jaworski took him by the arm and led him away.

Outside, Brooks came to Wallace's side. I know I'm repeating myself, but this really sucks. That poor bastard is going to jail for trying to protect his little girl.'

'It sucks more than that,' Reyes said. 'The Cortez family are all illegals. Miguel is going to go to jail. Manuela and Sara will be deported.'

'He was wrong for doing it, of course,' Wallace said, 'but under the circumstances...'

Reyes nodded. 'You're right. Sometimes a man needs a-killin'.'

Wallace gave her partner a puzzled look. Sal had been acting funny all afternoon.

'Just something my cousin used to say,' he said.

Back in the squad-room, the others were finishing their reports. Albanese told her that Kowalski's mother had been located in Alabama. 'Get this: the woman's a hellfire southern Baptist. Hasn't spoken to her son in years. As his sole heir, she's going to give all his shit away to charity – in her words, "using the Devil's money to do God's work".'

From his cubicle, Wagner shouted. 'Does that mean the porn tapes are up for grabs?'

After the laughter died, Wallace went up to Reyes. 'Hey, partner, sorry about your day off.'

Reyes put his hand to the bandage across his forehead. 'I understand. Of course, spending the day wallowing in the filth was fun, but putting an otherwise decent man in jail for ridding the world of scum topped it off.'

'Cortez didn't have to kill Kowalski. On the other hand, if he hadn't entered the country illegally in the first place...' She shrugged. 'It's crappy but we don't make the laws and we don't judge. We enforce the rules as they are given to us. It was a good collar, Sal.'

'Thanks,' Reyes said. 'Will Californians sleep better tonight because Kowalski is dead or because Cortez is in jail? What about Monaghan?'

'We had to cut her loose.'

'But she knew all about Kowalski.'

'Brightman paid for the lawyer. It was Siley's call.' Reyes pulled a grimace. 'Hey, your kid's bike was in the trunk of my car. I put it over by the door.'

Reyes looked at his watch. 'I'm so late now that Pam will shove that Barney bike up my ass.'

'I'm going home. See ya tomorrow.'

'You should all go home,' said Brooks. 'Reports can wait until tomorrow.'

Wallace walked to her car, sank into the driver's seat and exhaled. She appreciated the silence. No radio noise, no lights, no nothing. She dug in her purse and found the keys.

What a day. Despite trying to keep Sal's chin up, it had worn her down, too. And the sad thing was nothing at home would change that. *You take the job home with you,* that's what her training officer had always said. She should have listened. Back then, twenty years ago, she couldn't wait to tell David all about the fresh experiences each day brought.

Wallace thought of her husband at the hospital earlier. He looked good in his suit – impeccable. She could see that he'd aged much better than she had. That didn't bother her. But was he really the man she'd married? She tried to push the guilty thought to the back of her mind, as she had so many times that year. Maybe if they had had a child, things would be different.

Wallace stopped at the Wok 'n' Roll and ordered a takeout for their dinner. Opening a fortune cookie was about as exciting as it was going to be tonight.

29

Wagner hung up and considered Monica's invitation to come over. He thought about her beautiful dark red hair and all that she could do with it. And the whipped cream she mentioned and all she could do with that. *No, I've had enough of redheads for one day, he decided. Even sweet and naughty ones.*

He dropped his reports on Brooks' desk. 'Here you go and here I go.'

'Take it easy, Harlen. You going to the hospital?'

'Sure am – I need to fill in our wounded warrior.'

'Tell Kahn I said hi. I think you're the last one out of here tonight.'

'I guess I'm a little slow today. See you tomorrow.'

Wagner walked outside and lit a cigarette. 'Oh, baby,' he said as he exhaled. 'Did I ever need that.' He leaned against his car and searched his phone for the hospital's number. He dialed and was informed that Kahn was in ICU and not allowed phone calls.

'I'm his partner.'

'I'm sorry. I can get a doctor if you wish to discuss Mr. Kahn's situation. Or I believe

Mr. Kahn's fiancée is with him. I could ask her to take your call.'

Fiancée? 'No, that's okay.'

Wagner climbed into his car and headed for the hospital. 'Fiancée?' he said out loud. 'The dumbass went ahead and did it.' He considered the situation. It would be a while before they were actually married. People got out of engagements all the time. *Once he's out of the hospital, he can tell Angie that he asked her to get married while he was under the influence of drugs. That's it. Easy.*

He stopped at Roget's Wine Chambre and asked William to recommend a good, but not great, champagne. William threw in four plastic champagne glasses 'gratis for my old friend Harlen'.

Fifteen minutes later Wagner was walking down the third-floor hallway of the hospital. *Hey,* he thought as he spotted a shorthaired brunette behind the counter. 'Hello ... Audrey,' he said, reading her name tag. 'I'm going into room three-eleven to see my partner.'

'Please be quiet when you go in. I suspect that Mr. Kahn is asleep.'

'I promise.'

Audrey leaned her head slightly to one side and smiled. She pointed down the hall. 'Three-eleven is right over there.'

'I knew that.'

'Is there something else I can do for you?'

'You can tell me what time you get off work.'

'Why would you want to know something like that?'

'Remember that old saying about there's never a cop around when you need one?'

'But I don't need a cop.'

'Are you sure?'

Audrey smiled again, and checked up and down the hall. 'Fifteen minutes.'

'I'll check on my partner and see you in fifteen.'

Audrey picked up a clipboard and walked toward Kahn's room. She peeked inside. 'Are you up to having a visitor?'

Wagner heard a 'sure', and walked in. Kahn was sitting upright in bed, the sheets pulled up to the waist of his green surgical gown. His arm was in a sling. Angie sat in the chair on the far side of the bed, her hand enveloped in Kahn's. 'Hello, partner,' he said. As he passed Audrey, he whispered, 'Fourteen. I'm counting the minutes.'

She laughed and went down the hall.

'How the hell are you?' Wagner asked.

'Not too bad, really,' Kahn said. 'Sore. My head hurts more than my side.'

Wagner hugged Angie. 'I was talking to the lady.'

'Ah, good one,' Kahn said.

'I'm fine. Better than fine,' she said, and extended her left hand to display her diamond engagement ring.

'Whoa. Who the hell gave you that?'

'You already knew, didn't you?'

'I didn't tell him,' Kahn said. 'He's not a big fan of marriage.'

'I knew.'

'How? I never told you.'

Wagner told them about finding the ring earlier.

'When's the date? he asked, trying to keep his tone upbeat.

'We haven't set one yet,' Angie said. 'I think I'd prefer spring but my mother made a great case for fall when I called to tell her.'

'Worst-case scenario then,' Wagner said, 'is that I have at least eight months to talk you out of it, maybe a little longer if Mom gets her way.'

Kahn laughed. Angie frowned. 'You had better be joking.'

'He is.'

'Sure I am.'

'Hey. Thanks for covering me,' Kahn said. 'Captain Siley stopped by a little while ago. He told me that you saved my life, again. That makes two all.'

'I didn't save your ass. All I did was call the ambulance.'

'Yeah, okay.'

'Look,' Wagner said, 'I brought a little bubbly to celebrate your engagement.' He set the sack on the table and pulled out the champagne and plastic glasses.

'I don't think Donald can have any champagne,' Angie said. 'He's really medicated.'

'Just a sip,' Wagner said. 'A sip sure can't hurt.' He poured them each drink. 'I only know Irish toasts. I hope that's good enough.' He lifted his glass. 'May you always have a clean shirt, a clear conscience, and enough coins in your pocket to buy a pint. *Sláinte!*'

They clicked their plastic glasses and drank. Wagner tipped his down in one.

'Alright then. You take care now, partner. I'm sure you'll be back annoying the hell out of me in no time.' He hugged Angie again. 'I hope you know what you're doing.'

She laughed. 'That's never stopped me before.'

He shook Kahn's hand. 'Congrats. I'm glad you're going to be okay. You kind of had me worried.'

'Sorry. Next time I'll duck.'

'Next time he'll wear his bulletproof vest,' Angie said, stroking Kahn's arm.

'Okay,' Wagner said. Hey, you know what? I'm kind of tired. I'm going to grab me a nurse, go get a drink and head home.'

They said their goodbyes and Wagner stepped into the hall. Audrey was waiting by the nurse's station. She smiled, said goodnight to her replacement and walked slowly toward Wagner.

They left the hospital. 'Do you smoke?' he

asked as he put a cigarette in his mouth.

'Occasionally,' she said. 'I'll have one when I have a drink, or after dinner, or after other things.' She grinned.

'Duly noted. You don't mind if I have one now? It's been a damned tough day from the get-go.'

'No, not at all.'

Wagner flipped his Zippo and lit his cigarette. He heard a whirring noise and turned to see a security guard on a golf cart heading straight for him. A little amber light on top of a pole flashed methodically. 'This is a no smoking campus. Put that cigarette out...'

30

'Oh my god,' Coombs said as she pulled up to the entrance of the Vander Bosch estate on Kings Road. The mansion loomed above them like a Bavarian castle. 'That's one hell of a house.'

'The inside lives up to the outside, too,' said Reyes. 'It'd be a great place to live if it weren't for the Vander Boschs living there already.'

'I can see why you married her,' she said. 'That's a joke,' she added.

'Yeah. Old man Vander Bosch used to say his only neighbor was God except God's house was a little farther down the Hill.'

'So, do you want me to pull in? I'll be glad to do it but I know Pam will blow a gasket if she sees me.'

'I don't really care. I'm tired of jumping through her hoops.'

'Maybe, but I doubt that you want to start a war with her on Fernando's birthday.'

'Shit. It's twenty to eight. She'll roast my *cojones* no matter what I do.' He looked up the driveway at the house. 'Oh well, I guess you better drop me off here on the street. I'll walk the last ten miles to the front door.'

Coombs laughed and put a hand on Reyes' shoulder. The touch was unexpected – he felt it like an electric shock. Reyes sat for a second and considered giving Joanne a kiss. Nothing passionate. More of a thanks-for-being-there kind of kiss. He glanced up at the front of the mansion again. He could feel eyes glaring at him from behind the far-off white curtains. He looked at Coombs. *Another time, another place.* 'Thanks for helping me out.' He got out of the car and opened the back door of the Volvo wagon. He took out the present that Coombs had wrapped for him. Somehow, although it was last-minute, she had found Barney wrapping paper and a purple ribbon. He pulled out his own bike, as well.

'Hey, thanks again. For everything.'

'No problem,' Coombs said. 'You sure you don't want me to wait out here and give you a ride home?'

'No. I don't know how long I'm going to be. Pam isn't going to let me take Nando out to dinner, I know that. I'll bike home. It's mostly downhill from here.'

'I'll see you tomorrow then.'

'Yeah, thanks for today. It's been good seeing you again.'

Reyes parked his bike by a concrete bench outside the Vander Bosch gate. *Okay,* he said to himself, *here we go.* He watched Coombs drive away, then he trudged toward the house. It was a long damned driveway when you were carrying a Barney bike. There were so many stairs up to the front door that he felt the urge to plant a flag when he reached the top. He rang the bell and braced himself.

The door flew open almost immediately. 'Well, I see you finally managed to make it,' Pam said. 'You do know it's nearly eight o'clock, don't you? You are amazing. Your son has a birthday once a year and you manage to screw it up every time.'

It's only seven-thirty,' he said, paused, then added, '-ish. I explained to you over the phone: Donald Kahn was shot today. He could've been killed. We had others. It was a bad day. I know it's too late to take Nando out for dinner. Just let me see him for a few

280

minutes and give him his present.'

'You can't. When you didn't show, we had to quickly figure out an alternative to having dinner with Daddy. We ordered a pizza. He ate too much. Then we had his cake and ice cream and he ate too much again. His stomach hurt so he lay down and I sat with him until he fell asleep.'

'Can I see him? Sort of peek in?'

'No, you might wake him up. He needs to sleep and get rid of his tummy-ache, otherwise he could be puking all night. Of course, that doesn't concern you because you'll wake him up then leave, and I'll be the one up all night with him.'

'Will you give him this present then, in the morning?'

'It's wrapped in Barney paper.'

'Yeah. Neat, huh?'

'Not really. He doesn't like Barney anymore. What is it?'

Reyes suddenly felt about five years old. 'You know what, I think I'll take this back to my apartment and give it to him the next time he visits.'

'Whatever, but if its Barney anything, he won't like it.' She stared at Reyes' face. 'What in the hell happened to you?' Her tone wasn't quite so harsh. 'You didn't say you were injured.'

'I had to take down a suspect today who objected to being arrested.'

'Anything serious?'

'No, but I'll be rubbing BenGay on a few muscles tonight.'

'Good night, Sal.' She stepped back inside, hesitated for an instant, then said, 'Call Nando in the morning.' She closed the door.

At least she didn't slam it in my face.

Reyes stood on the Vander Bosch steps for a minute. He could hear Vander Bosch and Pam shouting at one another inside but he couldn't hear what it was they were discussing so loudly. He walked slowly down the steps as he considered what he should do. One thing he knew for sure. Pam and her dad would blow this whole episode out of proportion and poor Nando would think his daddy didn't love him. There wasn't much he could do about that tonight. Tomorrow he would call Nando and explain things. They would go together and pick out a bike. Then the two of them could take rides together. He knew that Nando would understand how a cop being shot was more important than going out for a hamburger. He was a little boy, but he was a hell of a lot more mature than his mommy.

Reyes headed for the street. He really didn't feel like riding all the way home, and carrying the present would be tricky.

He passed back through the gate, walked over to the concrete bench and put Nando's bike down. He took his phone from his pocket, flipped it open to call a cab. He was halfway through the number when it dawned on him. *My bike!* He stared for a few seconds at the bench. 'Son-of-a-bitch. Somebody stole my bike.' He looked around, feeling like an idiot, then kicked the bench in anger. *Who the fuck, in this neighborhood, needed to steal a bike?* Everyone who lived around here was Fortune Five Hundred rich.

Reyes called the station. 'Hey, this is Reyes. You have anyone that might not be busy? My bike was stolen.'

After the dispatcher finished laughing, she got Reyes' location and said she'd send a patrol over 'to take the report'.

Almost twenty minutes later a squad car pulled up and stopped in front of Reyes. He got up from the bench and walked over to the car. When he got about five feet from the door, the driver flicked on the spotlight and shone it directly in his face.

'Hey, hey.' Reyes said, shielding his eyes. 'Kill the light.' He held up his badge and waved it back and forth. 'I'm Detective Reyes.'

The spotlight went out. The police officer lowered the passenger side window. Reyes put his hands on the roof and bent over to talk to the officer, blinking his eyes. 'Thanks for coming over,' he said as he stuck his face in the window. 'I've had a bad day.'

'Jesus H. Cheesecake, what happened to your face? Someone object to that yellow suit?'

'Donawald?'

'And now you're telling me your bike was stolen?'

'Donawald, what in the hell are you doing on swings?'

Joe Donawald leaned over so Reyes could see him. 'One of the guys had to take his wife in to have a baby so I said I'd stay a couple of hours OT. I think Maxwell is relieving me at nine.'

'Well, how lucky can one man get? I get to see you first thing this morning and last thing at night.'

'I'm like your toothbrush, huh?'

'More like my toilet. Can I put my kid's bike in your trunk, please?'

'I thought Dispatch said someone stole your bike.'

'My bike. They stole *my* bike. This one is my kid's birthday present.'

'Why don't you ride it home?'

'It's a disassembled Barney bike, Joe.'

Donawald popped the trunk and Reyes dropped the Barney bike inside.

Reyes was grateful that Donawald was silent as they drove back into the Valley.

He thought about poor Nando lying there with a tummy-ache and there wasn't anything his daddy could do about it. His mind shifted to Sara Cortez and how shitty her life must have been so far and how it was going to get worse in the coming weeks. Nando may have a shrew for a mom, an ogre for a grandfather, and a cop for a daddy, but his life should be pretty good. All of his relatives loved him. And Grandpa had enough money to ensure Nando's future would be free from worry.

Donawald asked him about the day's events. The last thing Reyes wanted right now was to talk any more about the Kowalski murder, but he also understood Donawald's curiosity. Reyes gave him the *Reader's Digest* version. Even then it took nearly the whole ride home to explain the twists and turns of the case.

'Here we are,' Donawald said. 'Home sweet home.'

'Thanks, man. I appreciate it.'

'Not a problem. Hey, don't forget your kid's bike.'

'Oh yeah, thanks.' Reyes lifted the box from the trunk, said goodbye to Donawald and stepped onto the sidewalk. A breeze hit him and he realized the choking heat had finally released its stranglehold on the city. It was starting to get dark, the ocean shared its winds with the landlubbers again and he was home. He put the box down for a minute and stood there, breathing in the fresh air.

A man came around the corner of the

apartments. Reyes squinted. It was his land-lord, Mr. Bognár.

'Hey, der, Mr. Reyes. Good news. I fix dat air conditioner.

Son-of-a-bitch. Now the sun is setting and the breeze is back, you fix it.

'Thanks, Mr. Bognár.'

'You betcha.'

In the darkness of his apartment, the little red light on his answering machine seemed like a distant lighthouse. Reyes put the box down, closed the door and turned on the lights. Pam probably remembered a few nasty things she forgot to tell him. He hesitated playing the message then figured, what the hell? Better to hear it now than to wake up to it.

He pushed *Play* and to his surprise heard Joanne Coombs' voice. 'Hi, Sal. It's Joanne. I hope you don't mind me calling. I kept thinking about you after I dropped you off. I wish I could have stayed but, well, you know. Anyhow, if you need to talk, Poirot and I will be up for a while yet.'

Joanne gave her number and said good-bye.

Reyes stared at the machine, imagining the person behind the voice. She and her cat were waiting by the phone. She was probably wearing a robe and fuzzy slippers. Reyes smiled and hit *Save Message*.

286